Alexx Andria ~~~~~~~~~~~~~~~~~~~~~~~~~~~ nce
author wh~~~~~~~~~~~~~~~~~~~~~~~~~~~~~~~~~~
exterior b~~~~~~~~~~~~~~~~~~~~~~~~~~~~~~~~~ s
sweet but ~~~~~~~~~~~~~~~~~~~~~~~~~~~~~~~~~
and, of cou~~~~~~~~~~~~~~~~~~~~~~~~~~ om…or
kitchen…or ~~~~~~~~~~~~~~~~~~~~ end up—and a
guaranteed H~~~~~~~~~~~~~~~~~~

Want to connect

Newsletter: http://bit.ly/1D7mH9A
Facebook Page: http://bit.ly/1VK6d1L?
Facebook Profile: https://www.facebook.com/alexx.
andria.796?
Twitter: @alexxandria2772
Instagram: author_alexxandria
Website: authoralexxandria.com
Email: alexxandria2772@gmail.com

If you liked *The Marriage Clause*, why not try

Her Dirty Little Secret by JC Harroway
Unmasked by Stefanie London
Inked by Anne Marsh

Discover more at millsandboon.co.uk

THE MARRIAGE CLAUSE

ALEXX ANDRIA

MILLS & BOON

First Published in Great Britain 2018
by Mills & Boon, an imprint of HarperCollins*Publishers*
1 London Bridge Street, London, SE1 9GF

© 2018 Kimberly Sheetz

ISBN: 978-0-263-93214-0

MIX
Paper from
responsible sources
FSC® C007454

This book is produced from independently certified FSC™ paper
to ensure responsible forest management.
For more information visit www.harpercollins.co.uk/green.

Printed and bound in Spain
by CPI, Barcelona

Dedicated to the dreamers who have the tenacity to become doers.

Every success story started at the beginning of a long road.

Don't be afraid to take that first step...and keep walking.

CHAPTER ONE

Luca

MY NAME IS Luca Donato. You may have seen my mug on the cover and in the pages of *Forbes*, *Fortune* and the *Robb Report*, because my family is ridiculously, obscenely rich.

I'm talking Saudi prince–level money.

I could wipe my ass with hundreds for several lifetimes and still not make a dent in the family trust.

My family descends from Italian aristocracy—some royal connections if you go back far enough—and we've done well enough with our investments in Donato Inc. to never have to work again if that were our choice.

But unlike some in similar positions, the Donatos haven't grown soft with privilege. If anything, our wealth has made us harder, hungrier—all about the victory.

We decimate our opponents, and the word *no* really isn't part of our vernacular.

In fact, I can't remember the last time someone refused to cave to my demands.

Until a certain redhead came along.

The one I'd chased to the airport.

Ah, there you are, you gorgeous pain in my ass.

Katherine Cerinda Oliver…my runaway fiancée.

If Katherine had thought to blend in, that spectacular head of burnished auburn hair was her downfall. Stubborn tendrils escaped her messy bun to curl around her delicate jaw, teasing wispy ends that tickled and caused her to rub her nose without thought.

My hands itched to twist in those sweet, silky curls and bury my nose against her skull. Immediate hunger threatened to override my decision to play it cool. The thing was, she was so damn beautiful sometimes all I could do was stare. I'd been a fool to play fast and loose with her heart years ago.

Now I was paying the price.

Our marriage, arranged by our powerful fathers when Katherine was only a girl, was about to be *un*-arranged if my runaway fiancée had her way.

If Katherine had any inkling how difficult the last two years—giving her the space to do her own thing while I focused on the Donato empire—had been for me, maybe she'd be less inclined to hiss at me like a wet cat.

But that didn't seem likely, given that over the last six months, anytime we were in the same room together Katherine did everything she could to avoid me.

We were supposed to be working toward building a partnership, courting each other, even. But Katherine wouldn't even sit through a single dinner unless it was insisted upon by my parents.

And now she was running away from me—*literally*.

I watched unnoticed from the jet bridge, allowing others to go ahead of me to find their seats on the massive commercial plane. I couldn't remember the last time I flew commercial—preferring the Donato private jet—and I saw little to compel me to do so again.

So she thought she'd gotten away, had she? Believed she'd outsmarted the Donatos by draining her accounts and leaving without notice, paying with cash for every purchase, including her direct flight to the wilds of California.

But as our wedding date loomed—it was set for this spring—and preparations had hit a fever pitch, I'd sensed something was up. My gut feeling only deepened when our last dinner engagement had gone spectacularly sideways and Katherine had practically tripped on her own feet in her haste to get away.

And when your bride-to-be wants nothing to do with you…well, it doesn't do your ego any favors.

In spite of her bravado, she nibbled at her cuticles in her seat in coach, a habit my mother had never quite managed to drum out of her. As if hearing my mother's sharp reprimand, Katherine lowered her hand to double-check her seat belt was cinched tight.

Then she trained her attention out the window, though we were still on the ground and there was nothing to see yet.

That hair was her crowning glory. If she'd been playing it smart, she would've worn a hat, at the very least, but then, Katherine was a hothead, passionate to a fault and sometimes reckless.

Case in point: her decision to run away before our wedding.

In certain circles, I was considered quite a catch—rich, handsome, fit—but Katherine saw only the man who'd broken her heart when he'd been too stupid to realize that a woman like Katherine came along only once in a lifetime.

I had a week to prove that I'd changed. Starting now.

I peeled away from the attendants' area to make my way to my wayward fiancée.

"Leaving without me?" I tsked, startling her with the silky censure in my tone.

"Luca," she gasped in open dismay, her brow furrowing as her nose wrinkled, as if she'd just stepped in something putrid. "What are you doing here?"

"I could ask you the same thing, love."

"Don't call me that," she warned with a glower that could flash freeze meat. "God, you're like gum on my shoe. Go away."

Not a chance. "And why would I do that?"

"Because I don't want you here," she answered, cutting me a hard look.

I stared pointedly at her ringless finger, hating that she seemed to the world an available woman, when she belonged to me. "Where's my grandmother's ring?" I asked, moving slightly so other passengers could get past me, but I was already causing a logjam.

"It's too heavy and it's gaudy."

"It may be gaudy, but there's a lot of history in that ring," I said. "Once we're married, you'll only have to wear it on special occasions or when we dine with the family. Mother has particular expectations about gifted family heirlooms."

"I'm never wearing it," Katherine returned flatly, "because I'm not marrying you."

Her declaration hit me like a punch to the groin. She'd never outright stated she wanted to call off the wedding, but I should've seen it coming.

"That's a big decision to make. I hardly think making it when you're angry is a good idea," I warned, glancing at the people trying to push past me.

"Luca, you're blocking the way," Katherine said, embarrassed. "Just go home and I'll call you when I land."

"Sorry, that's not going to happen. Where you go, I go."

Before Katherine could hit me with a retort, the sharply dressed attendant made her way to us, her expression polite yet annoyed that I was standing in the aisle as she said, "I need you to take your seat, sir. Perhaps I can help?"

Katherine was really going to be pissed, but it couldn't be helped. "Yes, actually, my bride-to-be seems to have gotten the wrong seat assignment. I was just sharing with her that we've been upgraded. Can you help us out?"

Relieved to find the fix so simple, the attendant smiled and looked over my tickets, her expression breaking into a wider, more accommodating smile. "Of course, Mr. Donato." She gestured to Katherine. "I am so sorry for the mix-up. Your seats are in first class. We'll get that squared away right now."

"Excellent," I murmured, smiling apologetically at Katherine, knowing she wouldn't risk a scene.

"Upgraded?" Katherine's gaze flitted from the attendant to me, indecision marring her beautifully expressive face. Tiny freckles danced across the bridge of her nose and onto her cheekbones because she refused to wear enough sunscreen when she went out. She wanted to tell me to shove my ticket up my ass, but I knew she wouldn't, not with so many people watching.

"Miss, if you'll just come with me," the attendant prompted, gesturing again, and I knew Katherine wanted to murder me. I'd take the risk.

"Fine," Katherine finally relented with a sour look she didn't even try to disguise, but I didn't care. I needed more privacy—and legroom—than coach could provide for what I had to say to my runaway fiancée.

In a world filled with daisies, Katherine was a wild blood rose—willful and breathtaking yet dangerous with sharp thorns.

But even roses needed tending.

And Katherine had broken her contract by running. I could be a dick and just drag her off the plane, reminding her that our marriage was a business arrangement that neither of our fathers would allow to be dissolved, but that tactic would only make things worse between us.

"Sweetheart," I murmured, settling my hand on the small of Katherine's back as we fell in behind the attendant. I caught her subtle stiffening at my touch and I prepared myself for an uphill battle, dragging a wagon filled with cement—oh, and the wagon was probably on fire.

Katherine gave the attendant a tight smile and lowered into the luxury seat. "I can't believe you. How dare you chase me down like a fox after a rabbit. I'm not your fucking property," she said, crossing her arms and skewering me with the heat in her eyes. "How did you find me?"

I paused, accepting a champagne flute from the attendant, then answered, "Alana told me. She also said you quit your job at Franklin and Dodd." She'd been working there for over a year.

"Damn you, Alana," Katherine muttered, exhaling an irritated breath. "I knew I shouldn't have told her where I was going."

"True enough, but why did you quit your job?" I asked with a frown. "I thought you were doing well in their marketing department."

Katherine ignored my query and simply shook her head, disappointed in her friend's loose lips. I couldn't blame her, but she should've known better. I'd never understood their friendship to begin with. Alana was the stereotypical rich girl, raised with wealth and privilege. She was somewhat clueless and out of touch.

I thought Katherine kept Alana grounded, but I had no idea what benefit Alana provided Katherine.

Katherine rubbed her forehead, trying to ease the furrows in her brow. "Damn, damn, damn," she muttered before leaning back against the headrest, her jaw tense. "I should've just bailed and not told anyone."

"Probably."

She narrowed her gaze. "Thank you, peanut gallery. Nobody asked you."

"Does your father know?" I asked.

She cut me a short look. "Of course not. He wouldn't understand any more than you would."

I swallowed the insult of being lumped in with her blowhard of a father, but in truth, while Bernard Oliver had more in common with my own father, Giovanni, I was nothing like either man.

"Why California?" I asked, settling in for the long flight, trying to make conversation.

"Because it was on my bucket list. And it was far enough away from everything associated with my life in New York. And yes, that includes you."

I barked a short laugh even though I was starting to bristle at her constant jabs. "So you picked San Francisco in January? I hope you packed warm clothes, because you're going to freeze your pretty little ass off."

"I'm well aware of the weather. I'm not made of glass—I'm sure I'll survive. Besides, nothing could be worse than a New York winter."

"I wouldn't be so sure about that. The marine layer creates a thick fog that eats into your bones. I think I prefer snow."

"The point was to get *away* from you. Anyplace would've been preferable as long as you weren't there. Even a swamp. And before you start pointing out that I've never been to a swamp, so I can't make that assumption, just stop before you start. You've screwed up my entire travel plan, and I'm really not in the mood to hear your mansplaining bullshit."

I knew her well enough to recognize that she wasn't playing.

"You know, I would've thought two years was long enough to lose your quills, but if anything, you've only gotten worse," I said, reluctantly ditching any hope I might've had that we could pick up where we'd left off all those years ago—back when she *didn't* think I was the devil. "Jesus, Katherine, I thought I'd given you plenty of space to do your own thing so we could make this work when the time came to marry."

She stared me down, shaking her head as if I were an idiot. "That right there is why I could never marry you, Luca. You *gave me space*? We broke up because you were caught messing around, and to add insult to injury, your actions were plastered all over one of those stupid paparazzi rags. You broke my heart and humiliated me."

"I told you that was a misunderstanding."

"And I told you, you're full of shit. I won't be one of those women who simper at your feet and believe whatever nonsense you happen to be dishing out."

I bit my tongue. Arguing with her about the past wasn't going to solve anything, but I did point out, "I never asked you to be that woman," because it was true. A simple and vapid woman would bore me to tears. In all the years I'd known Katherine, *boring* was never a word I'd use to describe her.

That photo had been unfortunate, but I'd learned a valuable lesson. Don't let cute starlets sit on your lap when you've had too many whiskeys and not enough food. The paparazzi had snapped the pic because of the girl, not because of me, but it'd sold quite a few tabloids.

It was pretty condemning, considering she'd been kissing me…and she was topless.

My father had been outraged, my mother had been mortified and I'd lost the woman of my dreams.

In all, it'd been a shit day.

"Why'd you wait until now to call off the wedding?" I asked. "Seems if you were still pissed about that incident, you would've called it all off before this dramatic exit."

Katherine's blue eyes flashed with ire at being called dramatic. She couldn't help it—it was the red hair. The Scottish heritage was hard to tamp down. "Because you aren't the only one with obligations. I wanted to call it off then, but my father interceded."

By *interceded*, it was a fair guess he threatened to cut her off if she didn't go through with the wedding. Bernard believed in brute force to get what he wanted. When our households were joined together, the connections in the business world would grow exponentially. An arranged marriage today wasn't all that different from an arranged marriage back in medieval times.

It was all about the power exchange, the advancement of a family's reach and influence.

"I wasn't given much of a choice. I was a semester away from getting my degree, and I wasn't going to let everything I'd worked for go down the drain because *you* chose to be a jackass." She drew a breath and blew it out, adding with a shake of her head, "Honestly, I thought I could go through with it, have a marriage in name only, but these last six months… I realized I can't.

And I won't. I'm not going to live my life to someone else's standards. So…I'm out."

"It won't be that simple," I told her, distracted by a whiff of her hair as she purposefully turned away and a wash of memories hit me hard.

Hemlock trees and sage, the heat of summer, coconut-scented sunscreen mingling with her signature white-citrus-and-cucumber body spray and the feel of her beneath me as I took her virginity.

I could still feel her tight wetness clasped around me, the way she shuddered and gasped as I gently pushed myself deep inside, breaching her lithe body for the first time.

She'd been eighteen; I'd been twenty-two.

The way she'd cried out, her teeth worrying the full pink flesh of her bottom lip, seconds before she came on my cock, her sweet sex clenching around me, greedy for more.

In spite of the slight chill of first class, sweat damp-ened my forehead as I took a deep swallow of my cham-pagne.

Jesus, now was not the time to think of that memory if I wanted to keep my head on my shoulders.

"I'm not looking for an easy way out. I just want out," she said.

Time to move the subject to safer ground. "If I were going to run away, I'd at least pick someplace warm with a secluded beach and a well-stocked bar," I shared, clearing my throat and my head of the pornographic things I wanted to do to my not-so-sweet bride-to-be. "I mean, San Francisco in winter…kinda crappy."

"Perhaps if things don't work out for you being CEO of the Donato empire, you can start a travel agency," she quipped with a dismissive glance before adding, "I picked San Francisco because I wanted to experience the cultural vibe of a liberal city. Not because I wanted to get a tan on some beach."

I smothered a grin. She'd always been curious and artsy—a big film buff, Coppola to be specific—so I could understand why the city appealed to her. "Well, that's good, because the San Francisco beaches smell like dead fish and they're barely nice to look at, much less lie around on the sand. The homeless are particularly fond of the beaches, as well."

"I know what you're doing," she said, bored. "Trying to scare me off with all your negative press, but I don't care. It's time for me to live life on my own terms, and I want to see the West Coast."

"You could've asked me. I would've made it happen."

"I don't want to ask you or anyone for anything." She turned to me. "Do you realize it was never my choice where to go to school or even what I would study in college? Your family made *all* my choices based on what would benefit the Donato name when we married." She huffed out a breath. "I am more than a doll you can dress up and prop in the corner, waving and smiling as the perfect, uselessly educated housewife. I never even wanted to go into marketing. I wanted to be a veterinarian, remember? But your father deemed my choice of profession *inappropriate* for a Donato. So the decision was made for me."

I remembered Katherine's desire to work with animals. I also remembered my father's disdain for such a career choice. I should've stuck up for her, but I'd remained silent. At the time, I'd had my hands full finishing up my own degree and learning the business at my father's side. I hadn't had the spare brain space to fight Katherine's battle, too.

But still, I regretted not saying something.

Everything she said was true, but it didn't mean I'd had any say, either. I couldn't give a shit what degree she had or what career she pursued. Maybe it was my misfortune to have fallen in love with my arranged bride, unlike others in similarly wealthy families that treated marriage alliances as business transactions.

"So, you quit Franklin and Dodd. What's your plan? Become a vet?"

"Maybe. I don't know, but when I decide, it'll be my choice."

God only knew it would've been so much easier if I'd felt nothing for the troublesome redhead. If I'd felt nothing but obligation to produce a kid, I would've written off Katherine a long time ago, selected any of the numerous women trying to get that gaudy ring on their finger, put a kid in her belly and moved on with my life.

But I loved her. That was the inescapable truth that made it impossible for me to walk away without one hell of a fight.

"So…did you pack appropriately?"

"Of course I did," Katherine said, adding sardonically, "Did you?"

"I didn't pack anything. Whatever I need, I'll buy new."

"Of course." Katherine's gaze returned to me, accusatory. "I preferred my original seat."

"No one prefers coach over first class."

"I do."

"Was this the entirety of your strategy?" I asked, drawing attention to how poorly she'd planned her getaway. "Liquefy your accounts and then melt into the bohemian life of a hipster on the West Coast?"

"Maybe. As long as whatever I planned was on my own terms, the details were irrelevant."

"I beg to differ. My family has a significant investment in your welfare. Did you think that if you breached the contract, it would go without some sort of compensation or penalty? My father isn't going to let this insult pass without consequence."

Katherine fell silent. I knew she'd given this possibility thought, but she was resolved to follow through. "I'll have to take the risk," she finally said.

"You really hate me that much?" I asked, all levity fading from my voice.

It was the minute hesitation that gave her away and filled me with hope—maybe misplaced and wildly irresponsible hope, but hope nonetheless.

Before Katherine could answer, the flight attendant returned with a refill of the champagne. I preferred scotch, but since I'd already started with champagne, I figured it was best not to mix. I needed my head on straight if I was going to find a way to get Katherine to love me again.

"I don't hate you, Luca," she said, glancing away. "I just don't love you any longer."

I didn't believe her. One thing I'd learned about human nature was that strong emotion betrayed vulnerabilities. In the last six months, she'd done everything in her power to avoid being alone with me. If there weren't residual feelings messing with her judgment, she wouldn't have needed to avoid me.

Maybe I was basing my opinion on my own wild hope, but I believed she still loved me. Somewhere deep down she loved me like I loved her, but she was afraid to trust me again.

I could sense her agitation with her sitting so close to me; her fidgeting fingers gave her away. Memories of growing up around each other, falling in love, having sex…they were all in there, rubbing against the memories that hurt. It was my guess that Katherine was running from *every* memory between us.

"I know you remember how good it was between us."

"I try not to live in the past."

Ouch. "It could be that way again," I told her. "If you'd just give us a chance."

She answered with heavy silence.

I tried again. "Katherine—"

"I want out of my contract," she blurted.

"Excuse me?"

"I didn't stutter and you have perfect hearing. Let me out of our marriage contract or I'll spend the rest of my life embarrassing your family, starting with an exposé on your family that begins with how I was essentially purchased to be your bride."

She'd thrown down a goddamn gauntlet.

"If you do that, you'd ruin your own family, as well,"

I pointed out, narrowing my gaze, trying to gauge if she was bluffing.

"I owe no allegiance to my father. He made this mess—he can deal with the fallout. I was never asked if I wanted to marry into the Donato family, but then, I was only a kid. Who cared what my feelings were, right?"

I knew Katherine had as strained a relationship with her father as I had with mine, but unlike me, Katherine seemed uninterested in gaining her father's approval.

Resolve shone in her eyes, and I understood the hard line she was willing to draw to be free of anything remotely connected to the Donato name.

Her demand was like a punch to the gut. I'd never expected her to go that far. I could give her the world on a silver platter if she'd only let me, but no, she wanted fucking out.

"You're willing to go that far to satisfy a bruised ego?"

She shook her head, obviously seeing things differently than me. "You'll never understand, Luca. That, above all else, is why I can't marry you. When people show their true colors, it's best to believe them. And I don't like your colors."

My mother would fall over in a perfumed faint if a scandal of this proportion reached her little social circle. My father would lose his temper and bring all the attorneys under our employ down on Katherine's head for breach of contract. He would ruin her. She had no idea the fire she was playing with.

I'd done this.

I'd turned a sweet, loving girl into a Donato-hating shrew who found me to be the devil.

I couldn't let Katherine's broken heart ruin our second chance before we even got started.

It would be ugly.

That blue-eyed gaze slivered, sending spikes through my heart as it raced. In business I was known as a boardroom shark. I could sense the tiniest drop of blood before my opponent even knew he was in trouble. Nothing scared me.

Except the thought of losing Katherine for good.

"Give me a week to change your mind," I proposed, my gaze pinning hers, willing her to agree to my deal. I needed this to work. "If by the end of the week, you still want to be free...I'll do what I need to release you from your obligations to the Donato family without penalty, as long as you promise to keep the details of our contract confidential."

Katherine stared with suspicion, clearly believing my offer was pure crap. "You're lying. I don't believe for a second that your family would walk away from an investment."

She was right, but I planned to win, so the consequence of failure was a nonissue. However, I couldn't exactly say that without sounding like an arrogant ass. Instead, I said, "This isn't about an investment—it's about me and you. Give me a chance to change your mind."

"I'm serious, Luca. I don't want to marry you."

"You've made yourself perfectly clear."

"Then let's skip the experiment and just call it done. You go your way, I'll go mine."

Never. "If you're so sure your feelings won't change, where's the harm in letting me spin my wheels?" While she considered my point, I pressed my agenda, saying, "Give me one week," because I wasn't going to stop until she agreed.

The fact was, I loved her. I didn't want anyone but Katherine.

Now it was up to me to remind her why, once upon a time, she'd loved me, too.

CHAPTER TWO

Katherine

Was Luca actually offering me a way out of my contract? Was it that simple? Agree to spend a week with him and at the end he'd let me go?

Offering the deal went against Luca's nature—he was hardwired to go after the win, no matter the cost.

In business, he was ruthless and vicious. His reputation in certain circles was downright scary, and yet he was offering me an opportunity to walk, free and clear.

My belly trembled at the implication, even as there was the tiniest sliver of hesitation that perhaps I didn't want to be free.

Of course I wanted to be free. Why else would I have made such a bold move to get away from the Donato family?

Because maybe you wanted him to know heartbreak, too?

I shoved aside that annoying voice that seemed to whisper in my ear at the worst moments. I felt nothing for Luca but contempt. I wasn't going to hitch myself to someone I couldn't imagine looking at from across the dining table without wanting to throw the saltshaker at his head.

But even more so, I couldn't give my heart to someone I couldn't trust. Giovanni had taught his sons that fidelity was expected of their wives but was not necessary for men. The more I'd gotten to know Giovanni, the more I knew I wanted nothing to do with his family.

Especially after Luca had proved he was nothing more than a chip off Giovanni's block.

But I knew that if I didn't at least give Luca the appearance of having a shot at winning me back, he'd never give up, and I didn't look forward to the idea of Luca chasing me from state to state.

"What would this week together entail?" I asked warily. I knew without his admitting it that he, no doubt, thought if he could get me into bed, I'd melt like chocolate in his hands and stumble over my own feet just to walk down the aisle with him. *Not fucking likely.* The sex had been good—but had it been *freedom* good? Yes. I couldn't even begin to delude myself into thinking otherwise. Sex had been the one thing between us that had worked spectacularly. So the answer was obvious— avoid anything that put our naked bodies in close proximity. A slow smile followed as I tacked on slyly, "What if I said there would be no sex between us?"

He shocked me with an easy shrug, saying, "Then there's no sex."

Yeah, right. I barked a short laugh. "I don't believe you." Luca needed sex the way the human body needed air.

"You have trust issues, Katherine," he admonished,

as if I didn't already know he was a man slut who fucked anything that walked. "It's an unattractive trait in a woman."

"If I do, I do because of you."

He exhaled, the subtle twitch in his jaw the only indication of his irritation, but Luca did his best to seem reflective. "I've made mistakes. I was young."

"If that's your idea of an apology, you suck," I said.

Donatos didn't apologize. Every action was deliberate, good or bad. From Luca's viewpoint, he had nothing to apologize for. I could already hear his argument. Was it his fault that I'd given him my heart before he was ready? Was it his fault that I hadn't been able to go with him to that stupid yacht party? In Luca's mind, I'm sure the blame for *his* mistake landed squarely on my shoulders.

Since our breakup, I'd had time to figure out who I was and what I wanted in my life without Luca's blinding influence clouding my judgment.

"It's true, I probably do," Luca conceded with a modicum of humility that momentarily shocked me. "I can't say I've had a lot of practice, but believe me when I say I'm sorry for hurting you."

I didn't want a life with a man who couldn't take responsibility for his fuckups—and offering a blithe semiapology years later didn't count.

Where was his apology when it'd happened? When I was broken into pieces, sobbing my heart out, utterly betrayed? My lips pressed together to keep from venting all the frustration that he wouldn't listen to years ago from vomiting out. Why couldn't I let it go? Whatever had happened had happened years ago. *Live in the now, not the past*, as Alana liked to say airily, because she didn't give two shits about anything deeper than when the newest Prada bag was dropping.

But I wasn't that way. *Okay, sue me—I hold grudges.* Deep ones.

Especially when I was made to feel stupid and naive.

And that day, I'd felt dumber than a box of hair for believing that Luca Donato could ever be satisfied with only one woman.

I blinked back hot tears, instantly irritated that Luca still had the power to hurt me, if even in memory. I narrowed my gaze, letting him know that I didn't trust there was much weight behind his apology, saying, "We'll see," and left it at that, grateful the plane had begun to taxi. I needed the distraction.

The truth was, I didn't actually enjoy flying. Anxiety fluttered in my chest as the plane started to eat up the runway. I gripped the armrest tightly, closing my eyes as the plane lifted into the air, the power of the jet engines rumbling beneath our feet.

I focused on my yoga breathing—from the belly, in and out. Flying was safer than driving, so they said.

I had no idea who *they* were, but I had to assume *they* knew what they were talking about.

"Are you all right?" Luca asked, interrupting my belly breathing. "You look a little pale."

"I'm fine," I snapped, returning to my relaxation techniques, but now I was a little dizzy. "I just get a little anxious during takeoff."

"Here, take a sip. It'll help soften the edges," Luca

said, holding out his champagne flute with the remainder of his drink. I shook my head, refusing his offer. He gave me a look that said I was being childish, but I didn't care. I didn't need Luca tending to me, in any way. Not even if his suggestion would lessen the sudden tightening in my chest.

"I just need to breathe," I said, demonstrating my yoga technique. "See? In and out. I feel better already."

"Suit yourself." Luca finished his champagne and set his glass in the elegant cup holder until the attendant could retrieve it once we hit thirty thousand feet.

Thirty thousand feet.

Eek! If human beings were meant to fly, we would've been born with wings! Panic started to override my breathing, and instead of controlled inhales and exhales, I was suddenly panting and spots were beginning to dance before my eyes.

"You're so damn stubborn," Luca said.

I couldn't spare the oxygen to tell him to shove his opinion up his piehole, so I settled for sending him a dirty look. Damn it, I was going to have to take something to ease my anxiety, which I did not want to do with Luca sitting beside me, looking as handsome as he ever was, reminding me that I wasn't the only woman who had eyes in her head.

Jealousy, now? Luca made me feel out of control. I wanted to tell him "go fuck yourself" in one breath, yet when women inevitably gave him fuck-me eyes, I wanted to tattoo my name on his forehead just so they knew he was mine.

But he wasn't mine, because I didn't want him.

It didn't make sense in my own head, so I couldn't possibly explain my feelings to anyone else, which became readily apparent when I'd tried to talk to Alana about the situation.

"You do realize you're walking away from a gazillion-dollar family, right?"

"It's not about the money, Alana," I'd reminded her, flopping back against her plush luxury sofa the night after my last dinner engagement with Luca. "I just can't do this. All the rules, the obligations, the expectation that I simply nod, smile and look pretty... And his mother! I'm more than a walking uterus. I was made to do more than pump out Donato babies!"

"But your babies would be *so* cute," Alana had protested, picking up on the least important detail in my impassioned declaration. "I wonder if they'd have your red hair or his black? That Italian heritage is hard to override, but your red hair is something even Photoshop can't replicate. Oh! What if they had his black hair but your crazy curls? That would be fab."

I had snapped my fingers in front of Alana's dreamy gaze. "Focus, Alana. I'm not marrying him. I can't. Marrying Luca would be admitting that I'm good with sacrificing everything that I am, just for money. I'm not that person."

"You're so dramatic," Alana had said, rolling her eyes and reaching for her phone. "Have you seen Georgie's newest Insta post? She's such a bitch. I can't believe she had the balls to say that Carolina's party was a dud. It was way better than her lame masquerade debacle at Halloween."

"He broke my heart," I'd reminded Alana, dragging her back on point. "Remember?"

Alana had blinked, then seemed to remember. "Of course, darling. He's a dick. But aren't all men? Fidelity is a unicorn, sweetheart. A fun bit of fiction we cling to as little girls, but then we grow up and realize variety is far more fun, and even better than that is having the money to go and *do* whomever we choose. Okay, so you *think* he cheated on you, but honestly, it's actually a good thing because you guys broke the seal before getting married—now you don't have to cling to those silly, outdated and impossible standards. Besides, you were in college when it happened. Have fun, baby girl. And if you really feel the need to console yourself, do it with his money."

That was, *literally*, the worst advice I'd ever been given, but I didn't fault Alana. The truth was, as much as I loved Alana, her advice just cemented the belief that I would never fit into Luca's world—and I didn't want to.

When I chose a husband, I wanted someone who shared the same philosophies about love and marriage. Not someone who believed people were interchangeable and disposable.

"So what are we going to do in California?" Luca's voice dragged me back to the present, and I reluctantly popped an anxiety pill.

I closed my eyes, willing the medicine to work quickly before I freaked the fuck out and jumped from the emergency door to end up as Flat Katherine.

"I haven't agreed to your deal yet," I reminded him

with a weak frown, my heart still thundering in my chest. "I don't know if I can stomach spending a whole week with you."

He cast a derisive look my way to quip, "You really know how to punch a guy in the nuts."

I shrugged. Luca's feelings weren't my concern. "Just being honest."

I was grateful Luca didn't feel the need to offer a rebuttal, which gave the medicine a chance to calm my racing heart and settle my nerves. By the time Luca asked about the plans, I could actually think straight again.

"Did you have a plan when you ran away?" he asked. "A place to stay? Anything like that?"

I opened my eyes, feeling more confident and in control. "Yes, actually. I've found a cute hostel in Berkeley that's cheap."

Luca's distaste might've been comical if I hadn't been so irritated that he was tagging along. "A hostel?" he repeated, his lip curling. "Have you ever stayed in a hostel?"

"No, but it looked fine," I answered, enjoying his displeasure. "Not everyone needs the Ritz. I certainly don't."

"You know you have to share a bathroom with strangers, right?"

"Of course I know that," I said with fake sweetness. Okay, so I'd never done it before, but it wasn't a deal breaker. I was sure everyone was hygienic and polite. I'd been curious about backpacking since college. Hearing my friends regale me with tales of their summer travels made me yearn for an experience I'd always been denied. The daughter of Bernard Oliver didn't gallivant around the globe staying in hostels, especially not with students whose families didn't belong in our social circle. So, maybe this wasn't quite the same, but hosteling in San Francisco, testing out my new freedom, would be exciting nonetheless. "I'm actually looking forward to the adventure."

"Adventure. That's an apt word for it," Luca responded drily. "Unlike you, I actually stayed in hostels when I did a trip after high school with my friends. It was mostly a drunken crawl across Europe, which was fun but also disgusting. You've never stayed in a hotel with less than a five-star rating."

"Hence the adventure," I returned with a glare. "Don't poop on my plans. I'm going to have fun, and you can't stop me."

"May I make an alternative suggestion?"

I decided to humor him. "Such as?"

"Let me take you to Fiji. I can guarantee the allure of sharing a composting toilet with a bunch of hipsters will fade a lot more quickly than the experience of lying on a pristine white-sand beach with crystal clear waters lapping at your feet."

He knew I loved the beach and Fiji was one of those places we'd always talked about when we were younger. I hated that he'd remembered that small detail. I hated even more that a part of me wanted to say yes, but I wasn't changing my plans.

"I want to experience life like a *normal* person, and a normal person in their early twenties is usually *broke*.

A hostel is within my budget. But I can understand how that might not be your scene. Feel free to bow out. You're a little overdressed anyway," I said with a small smile as my gaze flicked to his suit.

"When in Rome, do as the Romans do," he said with a shrug. "Jeans and hoodies, it is."

"You're really going to stay in a hostel with me?"

"Why not? Sounds fun. Maybe I'll diversify my portfolio and buy one for a tax shelter."

My sound of disgust was followed by "Just like a Donato. Not everything is for sale."

"That hasn't been my experience."

"Life is about more than what can be bought."

He agreed, leaning over to whisper in my ear, "Life is about good sex."

I gasped, and he chuckled at catching me off guard. If he thought keeping me off balance would tip the scales in his favor, he was wrong. Even if his voice in my ear had just started percolating my blood with a heat I remembered all too well.

I swallowed, forcing a smile. "Yeah, well, we're not having sex, so…" *Keep telling yourself that and you might believe it.* It was absolutely essential that neither one of us was naked around the other—that was just asking for trouble.

"Let's make this week interesting," he proposed with a playful glint in his eye. "We will compromise—"

"Donatos don't compromise," I cut in flatly.

"There's a first time for everything," he countered with a small smile. "Are you interested in hearing my proposal?"

No. Yes. Well, maybe. "If only out of sheer curiosity," I answered, one brow climbing with skepticism. "What is this compromise?"

"If you agree to splitting our days between things I want to do, I will agree to do what you want to do without complaint. I get three days, you get three days, with the last day reserved for travel."

"Technically, someone is going to get shafted, because today is a travel day, too."

"Unfortunately, as you've already picked hostel living for our first day, you've used up one of your days," he explained, matter-of-fact. "Unless you'd like to change your mind about staying in a hipster hotel. I'd be happy to make arrangements at the Four Seasons."

I hesitated, weighing his offer. I could tell by the way his gaze intensified that he sensed victory, but he never made the rookie mistake of celebrating too early. He knew I was intrigued by his offer. I was even curious as to how he'd choose to spend his days when I'd taken sex off the table.

But I also knew giving a Donato room to wiggle was dangerous.

"Why do you care, Luca? Wouldn't it be so much easier to just walk away?" I asked, exasperated by the allure of the game beginning between us. It felt too familiar, too entertaining. I didn't want to feel anything remotely positive with Luca, because I didn't want to question or regret my decision.

Luca offered a brief smile before saying with a shrug, "You signed a contract. If being a part of this family has taught you anything, it is that you honor your commitments."

Not because he loved me, but because Donato men didn't walk away from an investment. I smothered my disappointment. "Very *Game of Thrones* of you, but I'm no Lannister—nor am I a Donato. You and I both know that contracts entered into with a *child* are illegal and, thus, nonbinding. Your family and my father conducted an illegal sale of a person. Even with all your money, that's still illegal—and despicable, I might add."

"Have you wanted for anything?" he returned, that tiny twitch returning to his jaw that gave away his temper. "Have you been mistreated in any way?"

"Not the point," I said stubbornly, shaking my head. "Still illegal."

"The finest schools, the best opportunities, every need provided for... Yes, I can see how you received the sharp end of this deal." He stopped me before I could jump in, adding, "And not to put too fine a *point* on your argument, but you were perfectly amenable to the arrangement until your ego was bruised. Suddenly, you were a victim and we were the devil. So, please, when you're forming your narrative in your head, be sure to paint yourself with the same colors as you've assigned everyone else."

No one liked to be called on their bullshit, and I was no exception. "Well, even the devil was an angel before he fell" was all I could offer by way of an excuse, because he was right. There was a time when I'd been blissfully happy, blessed even, not because of the money and the privilege, but because I'd been in love with a man I thought felt the same way about me.

"Better to reign in hell than serve in heaven," Luca said with a flippant shrug. "Let me know your decision before we land. Now, if you don't mind, I'm going to catch up on some sleep. Feel free to glower out the window, but do so silently."

"I don't glower," I muttered, but he'd already tuned me out and my anxiety medication was making me sleepy. There was no point in arguing an unfortunate fact. Yes, I'd been in love with Luca, and being his bride had been my favorite daydream.

But things changed. People woke up. And rose-colored glasses often broke under the pressure of reality.

I couldn't marry Luca—not if I wanted anything that was truly me to survive.

CHAPTER THREE

Katherine

IN SPITE OF the medication, I couldn't sleep, unlike Luca, who slept like a baby without a care in the world. While I tried to find a comfortable position, he snored lightly, deep in dreamland.

It was just like a Donato to manipulate a situation to their advantage in any way possible. I sneaked a glance at his profile. Dark hair, sharply barbered with perfect edges, his clean-shaven jaw without a single nick, as if even the blade was afraid of failing a Donato.

But I remembered a time when Luca wasn't so concerned with the appearance of perfection.

When he'd smiled with warmth, when his blue eyes had sparkled with mischief and fun.

I squeezed my eyes shut against the unwelcome memories that began to spill forward with the slightest encouragement. That was the thing about opening a door, right? Hard to slam shut once the wind started pushing against it.

"You're so beautiful…"

Luca's voice echoed, a distant remnant of a different time between two different people.

It'd been a humid day in the city, and my prep school graduation from Dalton loomed. Luca had spirited me away with a promise of a private celebration between the two of us.

I remembered everything about that day—the smell of the wind as it made my hair dance through the open convertible top of his Maserati—how I couldn't keep the hem of my sundress from rippling up my thighs and Luca couldn't keep his eyes on the road.

"We're going to crash." I'd laughed, gesturing at him to stay focused, but I was drunk on his affection, his seeming obsession with me. I teased him with flirty looks cast his way, knowing I was driving him nuts. "Where are we going?" I asked, grinning.

"You'll see."

I loved the way he took control. I always felt safe with Luca. He seemed so worldly, so accomplished.

Of course, he was the Donato heir—the expectations were high. Giovanni Donato had groomed him from the time he was a kid to take the reins when the time came for the mean-eyed bear to retire.

Giovanni scared me and always had. It amazed me that Luca sprang from Giovanni's DNA. Luca was nothing like his father. Luca was kind, sweet, caring and so romantic, whereas Giovanni was cold, manipulative and quite comfortable playing the bad guy if need be. To be honest, I avoided Giovanni whenever I could, which wasn't difficult, as Giovanni paid as little attention to

me as he would the multitude of servants looking after
his palatial mansion.

But who cared about Giovanni Donato, anyway? He
wasn't around. It was just me and Luca, and I was his
princess. The sleek car ate the road as we headed to our
unknown destination. The joy in my heart was near to
bursting. I was living the dream. How'd I get so lucky?

Just as I was about to scream from the building anticipation, Luca pulled into a dirt driveway lined with a
white picket fence for as far as I could see. Rolling hills
with gently swaying dried grass waved as we drove by,
and cows dotted the pastureland.

"Where are we?" I asked, delighted as we parked
in front of a huge farmhouse, chickens clucking and
scratching around the front yard. It was like the living
embodiment of "The Farmer in the Dell."

"I thought you might like this place," Luca said,
opening my door with a wide smile. "It's a sanctuary for
animals that have been rescued from abusive owners."

My eyes widened as I exclaimed, "Do they have
goats? Oh, please, say they have goats!"

"They have goats."

I squealed and jumped into his arms, wrapping my
legs around his strong torso. His hands cupped my behind as he laughed at my enthusiasm while I peppered
his adorable face with kisses. "You're the best! This is
amazing! I can't believe you brought me here."

Luca knew I'd always been obsessed with goats;
they always made me laugh and I'd tried, unsuccess-
fully, to get approval from my dorm manager to have
one as a pet.

I hopped down and slid my hand into his as we walked into the farmhouse, a permanent smile on my face. The old hardwood groaned in welcome beneath our feet, and the smell of beeswax and lemon was the most heavenly aroma I'd ever known.

"You must be Mr. and Mrs. Donato," a plump woman said, coming forward as she wiped her hands on the apron tied around her ample waist.

I blushed at her assumption, biting my lip at the wild thrill of being called Mrs. Donato, but Luca corrected her with a coy "She's not mine yet, but hopefully someday." I wanted to pinch him playfully. Of course, I would marry him at twenty-three, after I graduated college, but no one knew that.

"Young lovebirds." She sighed as if remembering her own youth. "Well, I'm Mrs. Ellering, but you can call me Iris. Welcome to Knucklebocker Sanctuary. We've prepared a special day for you and your sweetheart. Just follow me."

Oh, that sneaky devil had prepared everything in advance, and I loved it.

"I heard someone is an animal lover?" Iris prompted as she led us to the large redwood barn.

"That's me," I piped up, squeezing Luca's hand as I beamed. "I hope to work with animals someday. Maybe go to veterinary school."

"That's a noble profession," Iris said, pushing open the barn doors. The scents of barn wood, hay and horse poop immediately assaulted my nose, but I liked it. It was so earthy and unlike the city that I drank in the ambience. Plus, the fact that Luca had arranged everything made it extra special.

"Harvard," Iris called out, "we have guests."

A bald, wiry man in faded overalls and a full white beard appeared from a stall where a horse nickered. "You them fancy folk from the city that's bought us out for the day?" he asked.

I tried not to blush, but Luca answered for us both, saying good-naturedly, "What gave it away? My soft hands?"

"Oh, go on now, be nice." Iris waved at her husband with mock disapproval, but it was easy to see they were both playing around. My heart melted a little at how easily the older couple flowed together, an obvious by-product of a long, happy marriage. I tightened my grip on Luca with a wistful sigh. *That will be us, someday...*

I awoke with a start, realizing that I'd been dreaming and we were landing. Luca was already awake, his attention focused on his phone.

What a difference from then to now. Gone were the smiles, the laughter...the sweet, good-natured Luca who went out of his way to make me happy with an over-the-top gesture, replaced by this manipulative caricature dressed in a ten-thousand-dollar suit.

I absently rubbed at the dismal chord that twanged in my chest. If I cared, I might've mourned the loss of the man I used to know, but I didn't care. Disdain had replaced any pain that lingered, and I was grateful. Just as Luca wasn't the man he used to be, I wasn't the girl he used to know, either.

If Luca thought he could persuade me to forget the

past with this phony seduction act, he didn't know how much I'd truly changed. Of course, Luca probably felt secure in the idea that he could win this little wager; otherwise he wouldn't have extended the offer.

Time to negotiate. "I want our deal in writing," I said.

"You don't trust me?" He tsked as if I were being unfair. When I didn't budge, he relented. "Fine. Anything else?"

"Yes, I will give you seven days, but at the end of those seven days, when I haven't changed my mind, you will not only agree to end my contract, but you will not seek any damages from the breach and you will leave me to live in peace. I never want to see you or another Donato again. Clear?"

"If I can't change your mind," he repeated, but there was something about his tone that sent a warning chill dancing along my skin. "But I will change your mind, Katherine. I have no doubt that by the end of the week, possibly sooner, I'll be between your legs and you'll be gasping my name."

I sucked in an embarrassed breath, glancing around quickly to see if anyone had caught what he'd said. "I said no sex," I said with a sharp hiss. "Absolutely no sex. No touching, no sucking, kissing or licking…nothing."

His knowing chuckle undid me, and I suffered an intense need to run far and fast. It was as if he could sense that my heart rate tripled when he was around, that my skin heated and my toes curled inside my shoes against my will.

My attraction to him was mortifying. My dignity cringed and wailed, *Remember how he destroyed you without skipping a beat? Do you want to be tied to him for the rest of your life? Afraid of when he'll, no doubt, do it again?*

God, no. Then suck it up, buttercup, and get ready to win at all costs. I swallowed the lump stuck in my throat but held my ground. "No sex," I growled.

"Fine." He sighed but then added with a silky whisper against the shell of my ear, "But I promise I won't think less of you in the morning if you change your mind."

A tremble rattled my knees. Was I afraid that he was right? That it wouldn't take much for me to crumple beneath his touch if I so much as gave him one single opportunity? That if I did let him in, I'd willingly bare my neck for the slaughter as I sank into the pleasure that I knew he could wring from my body? Okay, maybe that part was a *little* dramatic, but my life was on the line. And as much as I hated to admit it, sex with Luca had been pretty good. Okay, *spectacular.*

True story—after one particularly long and exquisite orgasm, I temporarily went deaf. Yeah, that had done wonders for Luca's already healthy ego when I'd shared that phenomenon with him.

But no one had been able to deliver that kind of pleasure since, so I knew Luca had some skill.

Immaterial, I reminded myself when I started to drift. I didn't want to live my life as a Donato Stepford wife. I knew that for certain, and no amount of stellar sex was going to change that fact.

I just had to keep my eye on the prize—my freedom— and everything would work out in my favor.

I could handle seven days.

Lifting my chin, I held Luca's stare, reiterating my terms. "In writing, please."

There went that damnable smile again as he said, "I'll have my lawyer draft something immediately."

And I wasn't sure if I'd just made a very big mistake.

CHAPTER FOUR

Luca

TRUE TO MY WORD, I had a draft contract, simple and concise, emailed to me within an hour of checking into the roach motel passing itself off as a hostel. As Katherine perused the wording with the diligence of a woman signing away her soul to the devil, I wondered how quickly she would notice that the single bed in the room was quite small.

If she thought I was going to sleep on the floor, she was nuts. I'd seen toilets in third-world countries cleaner than this dingy, faded linoleum, and I wasn't touching it with my bare feet, much less my backside.

"Everything in order?" I asked.

A subtle frown pulled on her forehead as she double-checked everything. Her frown deepened as she regarded me with irritation. "The bedroom clause? I told you no sex."

"Are you saying you can't sleep beside me without tearing off my clothes and having your wicked way with me?"

"Please—" she rolled her eyes "—you know *I* won't have a problem, but *you*, on the other hand… I don't believe you can keep your hands to yourself."

Oh, sweet Katherine, you're going to beg for my hands—and tongue—by the time I'm through with you.

"I guess we'll have to see," I said with a small shrug. "Anything else?"

The indecision as she vacillated between refusing to sign and going forward was intriguing. I think of the many things I enjoyed about Katherine, it was her stubborn refusal to simply do as she was told. Maybe I was tired of people always jumping when I barked. I wouldn't put it past Katherine to rip up the contract out of spite.

Finally, she signed her name with flourish, chewing her plump bottom lip as she finished. "There. Done. You get one week and then I'm gone."

"So the contract says," I agreed, causing her to cast a suspicious look my way. I smiled. "Now that the legalities are out of the way…shall we discuss the schedule?"

Katherine drew a deep breath and exhaled with a nod. "Might as well."

"We can do this one of two ways. You can take all your days consecutively or we can trade off. Which do you prefer?"

"I prefer not having you in my space at all," she answered with a perfunctory smile. "But seeing as I just agreed to this ridiculous game, we'll switch off."

"Excellent," I said, already ready to vacate this trash bin. I would have the penthouse suite booked at the most exclusive hotel in the city for tomorrow. At the very least, I'd get a decent shower, which I knew wasn't going to happen here. "On to the second order of business… as you can see, the bed is quite small."

"I wasn't counting on company," Katherine said, but she could already see where I was heading. "I guess you'll have to sleep on the floor."

"You and I both know that's not going to happen."

"The contract says one bedroom, not one bed," she pointed out. "So, technically, if we're still in the same room…it doesn't mean that we have to be in the same bed."

"You can take the floor if you like, but I'm taking the bed," I said, enjoying how her upper lip wrinkled in subtle distaste for the same reasons mine did. "But if you're amenable to sharing the bed, I'm not opposed to it."

"I don't mind sleeping on the floor," she bluffed.

"Excellent. Then it's settled. Maybe we can get an extra blanket for you. San Francisco is quite chilly at night."

Especially in January.

"You would make me sleep on the floor?" Katherine asked.

"Of course not. You're the one insisting on sleeping on the floor."

"I am not," she refuted, scowling a little. "*You* are by not being a gentleman."

At that I laughed. "Have I ever been accused of being a gentleman?"

Katherine opened her mouth but stopped short. I would give anything for a window into that overactive brain of hers. What memory had popped in before she ignored it? I would ask if I thought she might admit it, but I wasn't going to waste the energy. Not yet, anyway.

"Fine," she agreed through gritted teeth. "But I swear to God, if you touch me…"

I waved away her threat. "Sweetheart, I promise I won't touch you…until you beg for it."

Katherine flushed red but managed a haughty "Like that's ever going to happen" before she left me alone in the room, supposedly to use the communal toilet. I cracked a grin at imagining how Katherine would shriek at the bathroom conditions. She talked a good game, but she was out of her element. As much as she wanted to play the hippie flower child, she was just as accustomed to wealth as me. I doubted the "charm" of her accommodations would last long.

Perusing the small room, I chuckled at the memories of Europe—young, dumb and full of come, as they say—me and my buddies traipsing through London, Athens, Paris in one long, endless summer of debauchery.

All those foreign, exotic women—I limited myself to nothing. Curvy, thin, short, tall, thick. And wild, shy and timid—I enjoyed the smorgasbord of female options and learned a few things, too.

We often joked it was a miracle we'd escaped alive with our cocks intact. Although Ryin had caught a particularly nasty infection that'd required a stringent round of antibiotics—but at least it'd been curable.

And speaking of debauchery…

I grabbed my cell and dialed my friend Dillon Buchanan.

He surprised me with a quick answer. "Fucking A, Luca Donato? What are you doing? Are you in town?"

"I am, and I'm looking for a little entertainment. You and your brothers still own that club?"

"We do—damn source of contention with the wives, but yeah. You interested in playing while in town? I could set you up with some playmates."

"Thanks, but I brought my own. My fiancée, actually. I want to treat her to the wonders of Malvagio before we head back at the end of the week."

Malvagio, originally owned by Dillon's twin brothers, Nolan and Vince, was an exclusive sex club, intensely private, invite only, and it took an act of God to gain an invitation from a sponsored member. The shit that happened between those walls was pure hedonism, catering to certain fetishes with a definite *Eyes Wide Shut* vibe to the entire operation.

The obscenely wealthy needed their diversions, and the Buchanan brothers had found a way to cash in on that need.

Not that they needed any money—the Buchanans were billionaires in their own right—but hey, nobody turned down more cash, right?

"Fiancée...holy shit. Never thought I'd see that happen. Is she mentally challenged?" Dillon joked.

"Ha-ha," I retorted. "Coming from the man who found a woman to marry him, in spite of being the biggest asshole in the city."

"I'm only an asshole to you. To my lady, I'm Don fucking Juan. What are your plans for tomorrow night? The auction is on the calendar. Interested?"

I grinned. Each year Malvagio opened its membership to women hoping to gain a sponsor into the club, but in order to do so, they went on the block and sponsors competed for the prize.

It was sexist as hell, but everyone seemed to enjoy the show, so no harm, no foul.

"Sounds fun," I answered, already picturing Katherine's expression of shock. "Put me on the list with a plus-one."

We exchanged a few good-natured insults and then said our goodbyes.

By the time Katherine returned, I was smiling like the Cheshire cat.

CHAPTER FIVE

Katherine

I DIDN'T TRUST that smile. Luca had something up his sleeve. I didn't expect him to cough up his master plan, though. All I could do was remain vigilant and deflect any attempts at seduction that he might try.

Oh, yes. I knew he was going to pull out all the stops. Probably try to woo me with fancy dinners and sickeningly trite flattery, because that was all he knew of me from our past, but I was long past that girl.

He'd broken me two years ago. And even before then, I could feel myself changing as my perspective of the world shifted. I guessed higher learning did that to you. He could waste his time plying me with useless trinkets and hollow conversation, but I was immune. I would endure this week and then finally walk away from the Donato family forever. Starting fresh was scary, but there was something exhilarating about the prospect, too. I couldn't wait.

A moment of disquiet intruded on my budding elation. I'd known the Donato boys as long as I could remember. Nico, Luca's youngest brother, and I were friends. I didn't care for Dante much—he was too much like Giovanni—but the point was, they'd always been part of my life. I didn't know what life would be like without their influence casting a shadow, both good and bad.

I guessed I would find out.

"I'm hungry," he announced, checking his watch. "Let's get some dinner."

Ah, here it comes. "Let me guess…a candlelit dinner for two atop the highest building in the city? A glorious view of the bay, stars twinkling, the mood just right… so cozy, so romantic," I mocked. *Like I'm going to fall for that.* I folded my arms across my chest, smug. "But it's my day to pick."

He frowned. "A simple 'no, thanks' would've been fine."

"Like you weren't angling for some romantic night out," I said, calling his bluff.

"Not unless you consider a burger down at the corner pub romantic," he said, his expression clearly saying, *Calm your tits, crazy lady*, but I wasn't buying it. He grabbed his coat. "You coming or not?"

"Not."

"Suit yourself."

My certainty faltered as Luca headed for the door. Was he actually going to leave me behind? My stomach growled in protest. "Are you really going for a burger?" I called after him, grabbing my coat to join him. He shook his head with open annoyance at my suspicion, then he kept walking. He exited the hostel and stepped onto the sidewalk, his stride so damn confident that even passersby took notice. I couldn't help staring just a little. Everywhere Luca went, he attracted attention. If it wasn't for his looks, it was his demeanor. He had a way of walking into a room and instantly taking control. It was as if the universe engineered every circumstance to his advantage, and that drove me nuts.

Even if it was a *little bit* sexy. Okay, maybe *a lot* sexy, but I wasn't going to feed his massive ego by admitting it. If anything, I would deny it until I died, just to prick a few holes in that giant head of his.

The pub wasn't far, true to his word, and I could smell the aroma of something delicious the minute we were within a few feet. My stomach clenched with hunger, reminding me that I hadn't eaten since that morning at Alana's, and I was privately glad I'd decided to tag along. I'd let Luca spend his money so I could keep what I had in reserve.

An Irish pub, the interior dark paneling punctuated by import-beer signs and raucous laughter, the place had a fun vibe that was hard to dislike. We slid into a cozy booth, and a terminally cute and bubbly waitress named Erin bounced over to our table.

"Welcome to Harrigans. What can I get you to start off with?"

"Murphy's Irish stout," Luca answered, earning a smile from Little Miss Easily Impressed.

Her gaze lingered for a second longer than necessary before she gestured to me. "And your lady?" she asked, clearly on a fishing expedition.

Might as well help the girl out. Do her a solid.

"I'm not his lady," I corrected her, shooting Luca a pointed look, daring him to say anything different, but the man simply sat there, waiting for me to give Erin my drink order, which only made me look like a bitchy shrew. "We are…uh…business associates," I clarified with a smile. "And I'll have a Guinness."

"*Oh*, my mistake. You two look so sweet together I just kinda assumed. I'm so sorry. Be right back." She beamed and bounced away like the human equivalent of a bunny rabbit with giant boobs.

"I think she likes you," I said, hoping to goad him into saying or doing something that would cement my disdain for him, but he didn't even nibble at the bait. I tried harder. "Supercute, too. Those boobs, right? Pretty big. If you like that sort of thing. I mean, of course you do. All guys lose their minds over big tits. I think it's etched in your DNA."

"You seem pretty obsessed with our waitress's breasts," he observed, amused.

Heat climbed my throat to heat my cheeks. "That's not what I meant… Oh, forget it. Never mind," I said, letting it go. He wasn't going to do something so overtly offensive as coming on to the waitress on the first day of our deal. *What an amateur move.* If I wanted to win, I had to stop thinking so small.

Erin returned with our drinks, and after we both ordered the house burgers, I fidgeted a little, unsure of what to do with my hands. Finally, I settled with my hands in my lap, but I was intensely aware of how an entirely too-small table was the only obstacle between us. Our knees were practically kissing beneath the table.

Was I supposed to make small talk? I had two settings around Luca—head over heels in love and despise with the force of an EMP blast—I didn't know how to be neutral.

And his seemingly relaxed, taking-in-the-ambience attitude wasn't helping things. Why wasn't he acting like he normally did—arrogant or patronizing—so I could find my bearings?

I didn't know how to reconcile that Luca with this chill *dude*.

"How'd you know about this place?" I asked, breaking the awkward silence. "Have you been here before?"

"Nope. Dinner locale courtesy of Google Maps. It was the closest to the hostel and had a good Yelp review. I figure we had nothing to lose, seeing as we were already taking our lives for granted by staying in the murder motel for the night, but, hey, life is for the living, right?" He lifted his bottle in salute and tipped it back. "Plus, it reminds me of a few pubs me and my buddies frequented in Scotland. Good times, except for the time I was persuaded to eat haggis on a drunken dare."

I dragged my gaze away from the spectacle of those sensual lips wrapping around the bottle top and focused on my own drink. I didn't care for Guinness, but it seemed sacrilegious to order anything less in an Irish pub. Besides, the beer helped loosen the tension cording my shoulders, so I continued to slug it down. "How'd that end?" I asked.

"With my head stuck in a dirty toilet and a bunch of locals laughing their asses off," he answered wryly. "Never touched haggis again."

I bit back a laugh, but I rather liked the image of a young Luca puking his guts out in a foreign country.

"You like that, huh?" His slow grin did terrible things to my stomach. "Then you'll love the story of how I woke up after a wild night in London to find my face a different color than when I passed out. The fuckers sprayed me with the darkest sunless tanner they could find. I went to bed white and woke up a mottled dark brown, and that shit did not scrub off easily. I spent the rest of the week looking like I'd caught a skin disease until it wore off."

At that I really did laugh. "Was this during your European pub crawl after high school?"

"The very same. How'd you know? You were pretty young then."

"I always knew what was going on. My circumstances weren't exactly normal."

He conceded my point with a silent nod, but before either of us could say much more, our food arrived and we both let it go, choosing dinner over uncomfortable topics.

And I was grateful. I didn't want to have a deep, soulful conversation with Luca about anything, much less my unorthodox childhood, thanks to his family, and he'd seemed on the verge of saying something distressingly nice or even apologetic.

I couldn't risk buying into anything he had to say, even if a part of me craved it more than I wanted to admit.

I'd long since stopped wondering how things might've been different if Luca had apologized in the slightest for breaking my heart... I wondered if I would've granted my forgiveness. I knew the answer— of course I would've. I'd been helplessly in love with the jackass. I was pretty sure stars had twinkled in my eyes like a cartoon character whenever he'd been around.

Hard to imagine being that way with anyone now— nor did I want to. I liked who I was, and I had no interest in returning to that caricature I'd been before.

Food was a great buffer, and by the time we were finished eating in silence, not needing to speak as we shoveled burgers into our mouths, I'd lost some of my prickles.

I felt more secure about making it through the week without succumbing to Luca's charm. I just needed to keep at the forefront of my mind the reasons not to marry him. Good sex did not a relationship make. I mean, it was important, don't get me wrong, but I didn't want to raise my kids the way the Donato boys were raised.

For one, Giovanni was an old-school misogynist, and even though Luca wasn't that way, his brother Dante certainly leaned that direction. I didn't want my kids around that kind of influence and keeping any Donato grandchildren away from the family would be near to impossible.

"Thank you for the dinner company," Luca said, patting his belly in the most comically unrefined way. "That burger hit the spot. Can I tell you a secret?"

My smile faded into quizzical curiosity. "I guess."

"I'm not into fancy food. Never have been. Most

times I'd rather just have a burger, fries and a milk shake, but it seems I'm in the minority."

"No, you're not. I hate fancy food," I admitted. "You remember that time your mom had the chef prepare duck in blood sauce? I thought Dante was going to throw up all over your mother's fine china."

"God, yes. Who knows what possessed Mother to have the cook serve that disgusting dish. Thankfully, she never did it again."

As much as I wanted to forget everything I'd experienced with the Donato family, there had been good times. My family was small, just me and my father after my mom died, and our home had always felt quiet. The Donato family home wasn't exactly cozy, but it felt fuller than mine. Nico and I had perpetrated some world-class pranks, but after getting caught one too many times, we'd realized we had to stop if we wanted to get into any worthwhile university. He was a good friend, but I was prepared to walk away from all of them.

The breath hitched in my chest when I realized the magnitude of what I was doing—walking away from everything I'd ever known—but I couldn't let myself travel too far down that road.

I had to do this.

But there was no sense in ruining a decent dinner, right?

We shared some light and totally safe memories, laughed a little, and by the time we walked back to the hostel, I was actually smiling.

Until we entered our room and my gaze fell unerringly on that tiny bed.

Could Luca actually lie beside me without making a move?

Would I be able to sleep with him smashed up against me?

I guessed there was only one way to find out.

CHAPTER SIX

Luca

KATHERINE PUT UP a good front, but the minute we crossed the threshold of our room, I could sense the tension in her shoulders. I wanted to knead the bunched muscles between my fingertips, hear her moan as I released the knots. But I knew if I touched her, all the progress I'd made at dinner would go down the toilet.

So I ignored her and went about my normal evening routine.

I settled on the bed with my phone to check emails, disregarding her completely. I pulled my shirt over my head and shucked my trousers. Katherine's sharp inhale made me turn in question.

"What are you doing?" she asked, gesturing to my near nakedness. "You can't sleep like that."

"No, I can't sleep fully clothed," I corrected her.

"I mean, you can't sleep with *me* like that," she said, her cheeks blaring with heat, even as her gaze kept dipping to the way my boxer briefs hugged my ass and cupped my cock.

"When did you turn into such a prude?" I asked. "I remember you being a lot less...particular."

"I'm not a prude," she protested. "I just don't want to feel your man parts bumping into me all night, that's all, but whatever. As long as you can keep your hands to yourself...I can handle it."

"No problem on my end," I lied, giving a convincingly real yawn even though I was wide-awake. Indeed, keeping my "man parts" from nudging her might be a challenge. My cock was already threatening to plump like a Ball Park hot dog on the grill at the thought of being next to Katherine all night. "I hope you don't snore."

"I don't snore."

"I'll let you know in the morning if that's true or not."

"The bed is smaller than I realized," she admitted, biting her lip. "You take up more than half of it."

"What can I say? I'm a big guy," I said without apology, sliding beneath the blankets. "Not much I can do about that."

"I know, I was just saying...it's a little small."

Yes, a California king would've been preferable, but I looked forward to a night with Katherine doing her best not to let our bodies touch. I suspect she would be so miserable by morning that she'd agree to leave this dump almost immediately, which worked for me.

"Close your eyes," she demanded as I plugged in my phone to charge for the night. Katherine stood, clutching her nightgown to her chest like a Victorian lady.

"Seriously?"

"As a heart attack."

I sighed and deliberately shut my eyes. She killed the light before changing. The mattress gave under the weight of Katherine's body as she slid into the bed, drawing the covers to her nose. "Is it safe now?" I asked in an amused drawl.

"Yes," she answered, her voice slightly muffled. "But don't you dare try anything tonight."

I grunted my acquiescence and rolled onto my side. I smothered a laugh at Katherine's rigid body next to mine. At this rate she'd wake up cranky and with a stiff neck. Hell, I would, too, if the springs piercing through this thin mattress were anything to go on.

But all in all, this was working out far better than I'd imagined.

Except for the raging boner now threatening to split my Jockeys in two.

I stifled a groan as I rolled away from her, my dick digging into the bed. If I could survive this night... everything would fall into place.

Hell, at this rate, I might not even need a whole week to have Katherine eating out of my hand—and sucking my cock.

CHAPTER SEVEN

Katherine

A SIGH ESCAPED me as the morning sun caressed my forehead. The comforting weight of a big body behind me, an arm wrapped around my waist drawing me close and a slow, even breath on the nape of my neck drugged me into a contented lethargy.

Something familiar yet foreign pressed against the cleft of my behind, and I instinctively wiggled, pushing against it.

A groan followed as the arm around me tightened. I wasn't awake yet, but I was slowly becoming aware. The tingle in my belly intensified as I arched against the sweet sensation of that rock-hard length pushing against me, insistent, eager. It'd been so long since I'd felt this wild need, this all-encompassing hunger to have him inside me.

It was too early to fight the need; my brain wasn't in control just yet. There'd always been something about Luca that had drawn me, even before I was old enough to realize how my future had been sold to the Donato family.

Before that awareness, Luca had simply been that enigmatic older boy with the devilish smile and the blue-eyed stare that made me want things I had no idea how to verbalize.

Don't wake up.

If I opened my eyes, I'd have to acknowledge how much I missed his touch, how easily I could roll to my back and open my legs for him. The feel of Luca filling me, stretching me like the first time—the memory taunted me. If Luca's fingers sought out my folds, he would find them damp and ready.

Pretending that none of this was real was better than admitting that I missed him, that a part of me still yearned for the taste of him on my tongue, still fantasized about all the things he used to do to me, how he'd introduced me to the tantalizing world of sexual pleasure.

No. Sex was sex. Orgasms were a dime a dozen if you knew what you were doing. Luca didn't have some special hold on me.

At least that was what I told myself every day, and I'd keep telling myself that until it became true, because I wasn't going to marry him.

My eyes snapped open and I tried to scoot away, but his arm remained locked around my waist.

"Luca," I said, trying to inch out of his sleepy grasp. "Luca…" But if anything, he seemed determined to keep me close. I gasped as he nuzzled the back of my neck, sending an army of dancing soldiers traipsing down my exposed skin. My nipples pearled to aching points, and I think my ovaries popped like a bottle of champagne. His tongue teased the smooth skin where my shoulder met my neck and I shivered, my eyes fluttering shut as my toes curled. His hand crept down my belly, seeking between my legs. Was he still asleep? It was possible. Luca was a deep sleeper. Or he could be wide-awake and playing that he was asleep so he didn't have to take responsibility for mauling me. *If only I wasn't dripping for more...* Suddenly, he moved, expertly rolling on top, his solid weight pressing me into the mattress. My legs automatically opened, leaving my core exposed and accessible.

Damn it.

"Good morning," he said, dipping to taste my lips before I could offer a word. His cock fit perfectly against me, the only protection between us the thin fabric of our underwear. He rubbed against me and swallowed my moan. The wanton, sex-starved lunatic hiding in my brain screamed, *Fuck me, Luca!* but I was doing my damnedest to shut that crazy bitch up.

Luca was the most masterful kisser I'd ever locked lips with, and that hadn't changed. If anything, he'd gotten better. He teased, nibbled, penetrated and commanded, leaving me breathless, all the while driving his cock against my sensitive mons, grinding until I was practically writhing beneath him, nearly ready to beg him to just stick it in already.

Where was my sense of control? No one touched me like Luca. Maybe I could delude myself into believing that the sex hadn't been as good as I remembered, but with his tongue in my mouth, my legs trembling with need, it was impossible to cling to that flat-out lie.

The thing was, I might not want to marry him, but maybe a romp for old times' sake wouldn't be a terrible idea.

I wanted him to bend me over the bed and sink into me, stretching my softness with the thick length of his cock. He could reduce me to a quivering ball of flesh with the talent of that tongue, and he knew it.

"I still remember the way you taste," he murmured against my lips, allowing only the slightest breath before plunging his tongue back into my mouth, evoking memories of how he'd done exactly that to my insides.

A groan escaped as he traveled to my neck, nibbling and kissing, sucking and licking, and I wanted to push his head between my thighs. I wanted to lose myself in the power of an orgasm only Luca could give.

Seriously, he was like a sex ninja, with skills that were damn near mythic.

For a brief moment, I was content to simply lose myself in the pleasure of being touched by Luca. My entire body yearned to feel his fingers and lips on my skin.

"Kiss me, Luca," I murmured, expecting him to slide down my belly to sink between my thighs, but instead he returned to my lips, plunging his tongue in, demanding and coaxing an equal response from me.

My nipples tightened to tiny, hard points of aching need as they rubbed against his chest, abraded by the thin fabric of my T-shirt.

His cock, rock solid and urgently pressed against my slit, teased me with the promise of pleasure. I wrapped my legs around him, desperately seeking that delicious friction against my clit. I was so aroused that I could've come from a single stroke of his tongue or even a few judicious flicks of his finger against the swollen nub nestled between my folds.

I couldn't take it anymore. I needed release or I would go insane.

But just as I was about to lose my dignity and beg, he rolled off and climbed from the bed to dress, leaving me panting, confused and disappointed.

"What are you doing?" I asked, struggling to catch my breath.

"Getting dressed," he answered, plainly obvious. "I thought we could check out this place called Mama's. Maybe get some banana pancakes if the wait isn't more than forty-five minutes. Supposed to be the best in the city."

"You want breakfast?"

"Yeah, I'm starved."

Two seconds ago his tongue had been buried in my mouth and now he was all about banana pancakes? What game was he playing? I should be grateful, not insulted, right? I'd told Luca I wasn't going to have sex with him. If I were an idiot, I'd assume he was being a gentleman by adhering to my wishes, but I knew Luca wasn't born with a chivalrous bone in his body.

So he was playing me. He wanted to pretend that he wasn't into me to prove a point.

Fine by me.

"Pancakes sound fab," I agreed, smiling with false brightness as I scooped up my clothes from last night.

I would change in the bathroom. "Give me a second and I'll be ready."

He nodded and pulled his trousers on. Luca wearing the same clothes from yesterday seemed like a sign of the coming apocalypse. He hadn't packed anything because he knew he could just toss down his credit card and buy whatever he needed, but still, seeing him so carefree was throwing me off-kilter.

I escaped the room, disappearing into the communal bathroom once it was free.

The smell of the previous occupant was enough to make me gag, but I was determined to put a good face on things. I couldn't give Luca the satisfaction of knowing that I kind of hated the hostel. It was definitely more appealing on a website or in a story than in reality. For one, my back was killing me from sharing that crappy mattress. I rolled my shoulders, trying to loosen up. I wanted a long, hot shower…in a private bathroom. One glance at the shower stall that had seen better days told me that'd have to wait.

God, I hadn't considered myself a snob until this moment—and the realization wasn't very flattering.

Still, there was no way I was admitting any of this to Luca. For all he knew, I was digging this lifestyle and I wanted to get dreads and a butterfly tattoo on my lower back.

And what the hell? Kissing and nibbling on me like that? That clearly violated our predetermined rules.

But seeing as we'd both been half-asleep, I guessed I could give him a pass—once.

I closed my eyes and swallowed the sigh that threatened to follow. The man had a magic touch.

Would I ever be able to forget how his fingertips felt grazing my skin? Not likely, if he kept doing it.

Just get through this week. After that, I can move on.

Dressed and ready, I met Luca outside, the bite in the air nippy enough to make me shiver. I probably couldn't have picked a more terrible time to visit San Francisco, but I hadn't been thinking—other than to get as far away from New York as possible. The dreary clouds hovering overhead were anything but cheery. Or warm. Right about now, Luca's offer of Fiji would be highly appealing—if not for my pride.

So, I'd just have to make the best of San Francisco.

"Mama's is only a few blocks. I thought we could walk," he suggested with a cheerful smile. He didn't wait for my approval, just set out with a healthy stride, leaving me behind. I hustled to catch up just as he started talking. "Man, it's been a while since I've visited the Bay Area for pleasure. In January it always reminds me of London with its damp and chilly weather. Just smell that bracing sea air!" He drew a lungful for emphasis. "Pretty refreshing. You're right, this was much better than some overrated pristine tropical beach."

I clenched my teeth to keep them from chattering. I'd always considered myself in decent shape, but my calves were burning along with my lungs, yet I was still freezing. "You can stop with the act, Luca," I gasped. "I'm onto you. This sucks and you know it."

But no, he was going to ride this out to the bitter end, I realized, when he insisted, "Not at all. This is one hundred percent me. I love the rain and the damp air. Makes me feel alive."

My gaze narrowed. I couldn't actually tell if he was lying. He seemed to genuinely enjoy our four-mile walk uphill. Who was this guy? He had me so turned around I didn't know which end was up right now.

Luca the uptight businessman had left the building, and in his place was…chill-dude Luca.

This had to be a game. Luca was trying to keep me tottering from one foot to the other. I hated to admit it was working. Not to mention, keeping up this pace was grueling. All I could do was huff and puff and chase after him. I had no more oxygen to argue.

We found Mama's, and the line to get in wrapped around the building and continued down the street. "Are you kidding me?" I complained, my stomach growling loudly. "I'm starving."

"Well, we came all this way. Might as well see what the fuss is about, right?"

I glared mutinously, blaming Luca for my burning calves, my pissy attitude and my grumbling belly. "These better be some utterly fantastic pancakes," I warned, folding my arms across my chest.

Luca chuckled, earning some appreciative glances from the closest women, and I wanted to bare my teeth at them like a wolverine defending its territory. *Knock it off. You don't want him, remember?* I drew a deep, calming breath and tried to find my center. "If you enjoy the Bay Area so much, why do you stay in New York?"

"New York is where my family is," he answered, adding with a shrug, "and New York is my home."

"Do you like New York?"

"I like some aspects of it, others not as much. But I can travel anywhere I want, so it doesn't really bother me to keep New York as my home base."

Yes, obscene wealth had its perks, I thought drily.

But there was something about his admission that gave me pause. Did Luca want more than what his family expected of him? I'd always assumed that Luca bought into the Donato empire without question.

Disquiet seamed my mouth shut. I didn't want to see Luca as *complicated*. I didn't want to look too closely at my own biases, because that opened a can of worms I wasn't ready to wrangle.

My stomach growled again, and I repeated, mostly to myself, "Those pancakes better be life changing," because it was far safer to focus on pancakes than anything else currently crowding my brain.

CHAPTER EIGHT

Luca

IF THERE WERE an award for ignoring a herculean boner, I would've won it.

I might've even suffered permanent damage from walking with giant wood trying to bust through my jeans.

But whatever the cost, it'd been worth watching Katherine struggle to make heads or tails of my unexpected behavior.

She expected me to try to get in her pants—and God knew I wanted to—but the stakes were much higher than satisfying a need to fuck.

I wanted Katherine to want me as much as I wanted her. I had no doubt I could get her in bed—that was an easy but ultimately hollow victory. Hell, I could've fucked her six ways from Sunday with her blessings this morning, but it wouldn't put my ring on her finger.

Overcoming her pride was the first hurdle to returning her to my bed for good.

I knew better than to try to sweet-talk Katherine

when she was hungry—the woman was ruled by her stomach, and right now she looked ready to start eating her way through the line of people—but forty-five minutes was a long time to simply stare at each other without conversation.

"Would you like to know our plans for today?" I asked solicitously.

"I would," she agreed with a wary expression, as if I were going to trick her into getting married at a courthouse. "Does it involve more walking? Because my feet are dead."

"No more walking," I promised her with a chuckle. "Since you've never been to San Francisco, I thought we'd do the tourist thing for the day. Alcatraz, the Presidio, etc."

Her expression brightened slowly with a smile. "That sounds fun," she said but added, "What's the catch?"

"No catch."

"I don't believe you."

"Katherine…you have to give me a chance to show you I'm not the man you think I am," I pointed out, mildly amused by her stubborn desire to paint me as the devil. I mean, I suppose in certain circles I was evil incarnate, but with her…I would be her white knight. "We could even check out the observatory, hit a museum or two…whatever you'd like."

"Really?" She still didn't trust my motives. *Smart woman.* "And then?"

"And then a little shopping," I suggested with a small smile, gesturing to my clothes. "Obviously I didn't come prepared to sightsee."

"And tonight?" Katherine pressed, watching me intently. "Where are we going tonight?"

"Well, first we are going to check out of that heap you call a hostel and into something less bohemian before dinner and a show. Sound good?"

"It sounds incredible," she agreed, but her gaze narrowed. "You're planning something."

"Even if I were...you're committed to doing whatever I choose, as it's my day and evening," I reminded her. I doubted I'd get much pushback on the hotel—she played a good game, but I could tell she hated the hostel, too—but if I told her about my true plans for us... she'd bolt. No, it was better to leave a little mystery. "But let's enjoy the day. I haven't been a tourist in a long time. This should be fun."

I brightened as I thought of something else to add, saying, "Let's check out the pier where the sea lions hang out. Those fat fuckers are pretty entertaining."

Katherine's gaze widened at my casual attitude. I guess it was my fault that I'd spent too much time in business mode, neglecting my future wife. I should've been wooing her way before now, but I'd taken for granted that she would be there when the time came.

Somewhere along the way, Katherine had changed from an adoring teen to an independent, way-too-fucking stubborn woman who didn't believe a word that came out of my mouth and was prepared to call me on my shit.

To be honest, the new Katherine was hot as fuck.

The challenge fired me up in ways I hadn't felt in a long time.

After an interminably long wait—I secretly agreed

with Katherine that the pancakes better be life changing—
we were seated in the cramped eatery/bakery.

San Francisco was a foodie town, and they were serious about their eats. I wasn't accustomed to waiting for
anything. As a Donato, I was seated at the best tables
and never asked to wait longer than it took to check my
coat at the most pretentious restaurants in New York,
and I'd forgotten how the other half lived.

But I enjoyed the wait with Katherine. The way the
morning sun kissed her crown, lighting up her face,
made up for the crease that seemed punched on her forehead. My bride-to-be was such a grump when hungry.

We ordered, and within a relatively short time, our
food arrived.

I was suitably impressed with the service, but before
I could sample the food, Katherine was already diving
in, stuffing her face with banana pancakes.

Syrup dripped from her lip as butter melted in a
gooey pool on top of the stack. Her tongue darted to
lick the syrup away and I nearly knocked the table over
from the instant erection that sprang from my pants.

She groaned with open delight, and I forgot about
my own quickly cooling breakfast.

"It's good," Katherine admitted, closing her eyes as
she chewed, savoring each bite. "God, it's good."

I swallowed and managed to drag my gaze away before she found me staring like a starving man who'd
just stumbled on a fresh deli sandwich. "Yeah?" I said,
clearing my throat and focusing on my plate. What the
hell did I order? Oh, right, eggs and bacon. Definitely
not as exciting as a carb-loading free-for-all. I shoveled

in a bite just to do something to short-circuit my intense need to lick the sweetness from her soft lips.

"You were right—worth the wait," she said with a giggle, the sound tickling my groin. "What do they put in these things? Crack? So good!" She paused midbite to ask, "Want to try?"

I looked up and saw her with a forkful in offering. How could I resist? I opened my mouth like a baby bird. Damn, she was right. "My money is on crack," I agreed. "That's unnaturally delicious."

"Right?" She laughed, returning to her plate. "Who knew the secret to happiness was to be found in a tiny, crowded bakery in San Francisco?"

I shared her laughter, returning to my food. "Maybe I could entice the chef into returning with us. I wouldn't mind this for breakfast every day."

I caught my mistake the minute the careless statement dropped from my mouth. I glanced up to find Katherine's smile fading. I wasn't surprised when she said, "*Us?* I'm not returning with you, Luca. I thought I was clear about that."

"I'm an eternal optimist."

"And I'm a realist. You get one week. No more. I want to be free of the Donato family, and that includes you."

"Thank you—you've made that very clear," I returned sharply, angry at myself for being so stupid as to lose my lead over something so trivial, but snapping at her wasn't going to gain me any points, either. I tried for levity, saying, "My mistake. Finish your crack pancakes before they get cold."

But the moment was gone.

I swore privately. I didn't have time to fuck around and play these games. One wrong move and I was screwed.

My cell buzzed with a text.

All set for tonight. Is your plus-one going on the block?

Any other time I might've laughed at the innocent question, but I was too irritated at myself for the stupid mistake to find the humor. I texted back, Not for sale. But we will be there to enjoy the show.

I could practically see Dillon's smirk as he sent back, Password: Bacchanal.

Katherine hadn't looked up from her plate as she finished quietly. All that progress…down the drain.

Back to the starting point. I tried for something out of my wheelhouse. "I'm sorry. I didn't mean to sound presumptuous."

Katherine inhaled a short breath, taken aback by my apology. I'd offered precious little of those in my lifetime, and she knew it. For the time being, the ball was in her court.

"I know you think I'm going to change my mind, but I won't," she told me quietly. "You have no idea how it feels to have your future decided by someone else—or worse, by committee, which is how it feels knowing our fathers pushed this on us. It wasn't my choice to be part of your family. Our fathers orchestrated this entire thing for professional gain, and I was too young at the time to understand the gravity of what it meant. I was sixteen when I signed that contract, for God's sake!" she hissed, running a hand through her hair. "But I'm not a kid anymore. What your family and my father did to my life…it wasn't right."

Discomfort mixed with annoyance flashed through me. I hated talking about the contract. I'd had nothing to do with it, and I hadn't been given a choice, either. The Donatos and the Olivers had been allies in business for years, and our fathers wanted to ground that in something solid and binding—the marriage of their children. I was the Donato company heir, but Katherine's father felt he didn't have one, especially after his wife died. Bernard could've offered Katherine a chance to take over the business. Instead, he'd archaically— with my family's help—groomed her to be a rich man's wife. And ensured it with the contract. Oh, she'd have a career, but she wasn't meant to be a CEO. Any children of ours—any sons, our fathers would insist—would inherit both companies and keep them running aligned for years to come. The situation wasn't pretty, but it was the situation we were in, and while I sympathized with Katherine, I couldn't lose her.

"Look, you've already conceded you haven't been mistreated. And you act as if arranged marriages aren't common in certain circles," I said, shaking my head. "Or as if you weren't perfectly amenable to it at one time."

"Yeah, well, I was naive," she shot back, her voice dropping to a harsh whisper, her gaze darting to see if anyone was listening. "Since having time to think about our situation, I came to realize that no one has the right to barter someone else's future. Wouldn't you rather choose your own wife instead of having your father dictate to you who you'll marry?"

The words burned on my tongue to admit that it didn't matter that my father had orchestrated the contract between us—I would've married her without a contract—but I doubted she'd believe me. She would probably think I'd say anything to get what I wanted, which under any other circumstance might be accurate, but I wouldn't lie to Katherine.

"The world we live in isn't like that of normal people, no matter how much you wish it was. This is our life, Katherine," I replied, unable to stop the chill from frosting my tone. I didn't enjoy being schooled, not by her, not by anyone. "And we are not free from our obligations."

"You're hopeless," Katherine said, giving up. "I don't know why I thought you might be different from the rest of your family. Thanks for reminding me that you're cut from the same cloth."

I might have caught the sheen of tears in her eyes or it might've been my imagination, but it didn't matter. Katherine didn't stick around long enough for me to solve the mystery.

CHAPTER NINE

Katherine

IT'S A BLESSING, I told myself, each angry step more force-ful than the next as I left the eatery. Better to know now that Luca still viewed this as an obligation that couldn't be questioned. He was incapable of seeing my perspec-tive, both in terms of the contract and when it came to a lifestyle other than the one we were raised in.

Yes, I went to an exclusive school. Yes, I was blessed with an incredible education, but I'd used that to get a taste of what life was like outside the Donato circles. All through college, I'd kept myself on a reasonable bud-get, not dipping into my trust fund when I went over it. Even when I was desperate for decent food, I told myself other students didn't have that luxury. I wanted to see if I could live more modestly. And it turned out I could.

I wanted to do something worthwhile with my life, not spend it lunching and one-upping each other with mate-rial goods. I wanted to work with animals, find a small, cozy apartment and enjoy love without the expectations and petty judgment of those typical of wealthy circles. I wanted something genuine—not the facade.

At one time, I'd thought Luca was different, too. Before he'd started working for Giovanni. The more time Luca had spent climbing the corporate ladder (granted, he was the heir to the empire, so the climb probably wasn't arduous), the less I recognized him.

He became closed off. He'd put in long days with Giovanni and be too distracted or too worn-out to talk after. The cunning business sense his father bragged about seemed at odds with Luca's compassionate nature. Unlike Giovanni, Luca had a kind heart. Giovanni never would've orchestrated something as touching as Luca's trip to the animal sanctuary because he didn't place any value on sentiment. But not Luca. Luca had always been Giovanni's opposite. Even so, self-doubt weighed on me while I worked through a degree my heart wasn't in. I needed him and he wasn't there.

The incident at the yacht party with that starlet was just the final straw. And when he didn't apologize, it proved his true colors.

I wanted Luca to be different. Maybe that was why it hurt so much that he wasn't.

I wanted Luca to be the man I'd foolishly believed he was when I was younger. Kind, generous, funny... compassionate...

It was foolish to wish he was someone else, but sometimes I thought I caught glimpses—especially when he was out of his usual element—like today, wearing yesterday's trousers, looking wrinkled and adorably disheveled from sleeping in the world's worst bed. And yet somehow still managing to find the most amazing place to eat on such short notice.

Yeah, he was charming when he wanted to be.

But it was all an act. That was the lesson I'd learned years ago, and I didn't really see the need for a refresher course. If I was still that love-struck girl, I'd pin my hopes on the flimsy possibility that Luca had real feelings for me—but I wasn't that girl.

I knew Luca was trying to live up to his father's expectations. Giovanni and my father—not necessarily Luca—wanted this union. That point had been hammered home with painful precision.

It didn't take long for Luca to catch up to me outside the restaurant.

"Caught your second wind?" he joked, his long stride matching my short, angry one. "Are we training for a five-K?"

"Stop, Luca," I demanded, skidding to a halt. "I don't feel like playing this game. We are not friends. We are not lovers. We are *nothing*. Got it?"

"Wrong." He surprised me with a twist of his lips that was both sexy and dangerous at the same time. He closed the distance between us, and I didn't have the good sense to back away. "You are my fiancée until the end of this week. When my time is up, we'll see where the chips fall. Until then, you're my bride-to-be."

I opened my mouth to shoot him down, but he grabbed me by the waist and jerked me to him, stealing a kiss as brazenly as a thief in broad daylight. My knees threatened to buckle. I instinctively clutched his shoulders, my mouth opening under the onslaught of his lips.

Luca's tongue darted, going straight for mine—taking, not asking. The shivers started immediately, mocking my weak protests until they were a memory. This was what I feared most—losing myself to the pleasure that only Luca could give, forgetting why it was crucial that I free myself from the Donato golden cage.

Luca was the jailer, even if he presented me with diamond-crusted handcuffs.

Even knowing all that, I was helpless to stop him, because a part of me desperately yearned for the bliss I found in his arms.

Luca nipped my bottom lip as he slowly pulled away, his grip still holding me tight. "One week, my love," he murmured, my foolish heart skipping a beat at the endearment. "You owe me one week…and the terms are nonnegotiable."

I wanted to blurt, *Screw the deal!* but I didn't. There was something in his eyes that invited no argument. Luca had never been a bully, but neither was he a pushover. Tension pulsed around us, weaving a sultry web, tightening until I could barely breathe. He knuckled my chin, forcing my stare. "Are we clear?"

I swallowed but managed a short nod. "One week."

A slow smile spread across his lips before he dipped to taste me again.

When he released me, we were both breathing hard. It didn't matter that we were standing on a busy city sidewalk, parting people like Moses and the Red Sea as they went around us. For a brief, heart-stopping moment, it was only him and me.

I wiped at my mouth as reality returned. Luca would

use every second of the week to try to convince me to marry him. Perhaps in addition to his need to please his father, it was a game and his pride was on the line. It couldn't possibly be because he truly did love me.

I wouldn't entertain something so foolish.

But I could do this kicking and screaming, fighting the entire way, or I could concede for the sake of a smoother ride to the end. Could I beat Luca at his own game? Could I shut off my heart and play the part of his fiancée, knowing full well I intended to walk away when it was all done?

Honest answer? I wasn't sure. I wanted to be strong enough to follow through with my plan, but there was a part of me that still yearned for what I'd thought I was getting when I was sixteen.

God, I'd loved him so hard.

They always said first love was the most powerful. Win or lose, the experience left a mark. I would bear Luca's mark on my soul until I died.

Dramatic? Perhaps, but there was no other way to explain the hold he had on me.

Time to forget all that. Time to play to win.

"Okay, Luca," I finally said, my tongue darting to taste where his lips had been. "I will stop fighting you on this and play the part of your fiancée until our deal is up. Where to next, *honey*?"

He slipped his hand into mine, answering, "On to Alcatraz, then shopping. I have a few places in mind, and I think you're going to love them."

I forced a smile and allowed him to pull me along, keeping step with his stride.

From the outside looking in, we might've looked like lovebirds out on the town, but I knew the truth.

At least… *I think I do.*

CHAPTER TEN

Luca

I DIDN'T TRUST Katherine to accept our deal without argument for the rest of the week. My fiancée wasn't malleable or meek, and knowing she would tell me to shove it was invigorating.

I know—stupid—but she captivated me in a way I couldn't explain, not to my father, not to myself. All I knew was I would do anything to keep her.

If that meant lying, deceiving, strong-arming… I was beneath nothing, but if she wanted to play games with the master, I'd certainly indulge her. She thought that by playing the part of the sweet fiancée, she'd play me, then walk.

I would never let her walk.

But if she expected me to play fair, she was naive.

My cock hardened at the thought of tonight.

The moment Katherine walked over the threshold of Malvagio, the sensory overload would start.

Sights, smells, sounds—the club was a smorgasbord of consensual debauchery.

Katherine was a powder keg of repressed need. All it would take was a spark and she'd ignite. And I fully planned to be the one holding the match.

Maybe it was playing dirty to push all her buttons at once, but I didn't have the luxury of slowly wooing her. Seduction was my best chance.

Once on the ferry to Alcatraz Island, the wind whipping her hair across her face, I pulled her into my arms to shield her from the bracing cold. She shivered and settled against me, choosing warmth over pride. Her scent teased my senses; her soft behind pressed against my groin. I sprang an erection nearly immediately, and I didn't try to hide it. If anything, I pulled her closer so that she knew exactly how she affected me.

Her sharp inhale told me she knew.

I leaned down to whisper against the shell of her ear, "You have the best ass. The memory of bending you over the bathroom counter...sliding my hard cock into you...it still turns me on to this day."

Katherine swallowed but recovered enough to quip, "Hold on to that... No repeats are scheduled on this trip."

I laughed, knowing she was struggling. Her shallow breath and the restless wiggle of her backside against my cock was evidence enough that she was lying through her teeth, but I enjoyed the chase.

Pressing, I said, "That's a shame. You have the sweetest O face. The way your toes curl and your mouth goes slack, your eyes squeeze shut as your breath is held captive in your lungs...it's the hottest thing I've ever seen. When I jerk off...it's your face I picture."

"Do you kiss your mother with that mouth?" she shot back, her tone breathless.

"I haven't kissed my mother since I was ten," I told her, allowing my mouth to drift down the column of her neck. "But I remember the way you taste. The sweet tang of your pussy haunts my dreams. The way your belly trembles and your thighs quake when you reach your climax…the way you gush, flooding my mouth when you come…your taste is an addiction I can't quite quit."

"Stop," she demanded, but the word was weak at best. "No sex."

"Who's having sex?" I questioned with false innocence. "We're just talking."

"But you're talking about sex."

"*Ah*, well, you never said we couldn't talk about sex," I reminded her, neatly snaring my little spitfire with her own words. "Now, where was I? Ah, yes, the scent of you on my cock…teasing me throughout the day, reminding me of how perfectly I fit inside you…the way you moan, clutching the bedsheets as you come hard… yeah, definitely my favorite memory."

"Luca…"

I ignored her plea. The ferry was moderately full, the nasty weather having put off many of the tourists hoping to see the infamous prison island, but there were enough people to make touching impossible and I wanted to slip my hands down the front of her pants to see if her core was as wet as I believed it would be.

The inability to do as I pleased only heightened the

anticipation for tonight. I savored my own frustration as I continued to stoke hers.

"Do you think of me when you touch yourself?"

Her quick no was telling.

I sighed, tightening my hold around her waist, my thumb lightly stroking her belly over her sweater. "Want to know what I think? I think when you close your eyes at night, your hand drifting down to your dripping pussy, you finger yourself with me in mind. I think you come with my name on your lips."

"You have quite the imagination," she said, glancing around the ferry to see if anyone was listening. "I don't think of you at all."

"No?"

"Nope." She added with a sniff, "I have slept with other men, you know."

I stiffened. "Careful." Unlike my family, I hadn't expected Katherine to remain celibate until I married her, but I didn't want her past lovers rubbed in my face.

But I realized my mistake too late.

"Oh, yes, when I really want to get off, I think of—"

I turned her roughly to face me. "You like to live dangerously," I said, my tone low, daring her to continue. The more I thought of someone else with Katherine, the more I wanted to break something. "Don't let your mouth overload your pretty ass."

Her angelic smile was anything but. "Jealous?"

"Territorial."

"Is there a difference?"

"Jealousy is an emotion reserved for those who want but can't have. Territorial is the need to protect what is already yours." Katherine held my stare, her chin lifting in a subtle motion. Defiance flitted through that expressive face, but she remained silent. "Make no mistake, Katherine, you are mine," I murmured, brushing my lips across hers. "Always."

The tiny shiver in her frame was the only confirmation I needed. She talked a big game, but Katherine was a quivering ball of need, her body reacting to mine with delicious readiness, no matter how vehemently she protested.

"Alcatraz Island," the ferry operator called out, and Katherine wasted no time in scuttling down the ramp, putting distance between us.

But it was the quick glance backward that did her in.

Her cheeks flushed, her beautiful eyes wide, her sensual mouth plump from my kiss…she wasn't running from me. She was running from the desperate hunger she couldn't deny.

A slow answering smile curved my mouth.

Victory was a dish best savored slowly, so as to fully appreciate its subtle nuances.

Tonight couldn't come fast enough.

CHAPTER ELEVEN

Katherine

I DIDN'T KNOW what scared me more—Luca's steadfast assurance that he would win or my fear that I might want him to.

I was grateful for the distraction of the Alcatraz tour so I could get my bearings again. Being pressed against Luca was hazardous to my resolve. The memory of each sculpted hill and valley of his physique was imprinted on my brain. My knees seemed to be made of jelly when he touched me.

But as we walked the tour, our attention drawn to the historical facts of the most infamous prison of its time, the tension coiled in my gut slowly lessened.

"To be locked up in this place…it must've been awful," I murmured, peering into the cell on display, the metal cot with its thin, worn mattress, the saddest thing I'd ever seen. Some of the most dangerous criminals in the United States had been housed here at one time. Luca was similarly engaged with the self-guided tour, his brow furrowed with interest as we listened through our headphones, and I took a private moment to regard him without his knowledge. Why was the man so beautiful? His skin glowed with his Italian heritage; his nose, strong and firm as his jaw, spoke of authority and inborn confidence.

Luca was hard to forget—even harder to push away when he wanted to stay.

But I had to steel myself against the onslaught of feelings that came into play whenever Luca was involved. The fact that he was playing to win only pinched harder. Why hadn't he cared this much when he'd broken my heart?

He hadn't tried very hard at all back then. If anything, he'd seemed irritated by my refusal to believe his thinly patched-together excuse. His clichéd "It isn't what it looks like" had been an insult to my intelligence.

Tears stung my eyes. I wiped them away quickly. Why did I care? I might have wanted Luca's love at one point, but I didn't anymore. Now he was just a threat to my freedom.

I thanked the part of me that was still looking out for my best interests, instead of the part that just wanted to open my legs and feel him inside me again.

The self-guided tour ended, and we found ourselves back at the gift shop. I was prepared to walk back out, choosing not to purchase anything to commemorate this trip, but Luca was on a buying spree.

He grabbed two sweatshirts, a ball cap, several key chains, two coffee mugs and a handful of Alcatraz-themed T-shirts. When I gaped, he just grinned and donned the ball cap with a charming grin, saying,

"This is how places like this survive. Gotta keep history alive." After paying for his purchases, he handed a wad of cash to the astonished docent, tipping the ball cap with a charming "Keep up the good work. The tour was great" before exiting the gift shop.

"Th-thank you," the guide stammered with a delighted smile. "What a generous donation! Alcatraz thanks you!"

I flashed a quick smile and followed him out. "That was unexpected of you," I said, standing beside him on the bluff overlooking the cold Pacific. "How much did you just give as a donation?"

He shrugged. "Just whatever I had in my billfold. Probably five hundred. I think when I get home I'll make a bigger donation. Places like this need support in order to make it."

The crust around my heart cracked a little bit, but I just nodded and left it at that. I suppose it didn't matter if his donation was all part of his scheme to seduce me, because historically relevant places *did* need donations to survive, so I let it be.

The ferry came to return us to the city, and Luca had a sleek town car waiting at the pier.

I was secretly relieved to have a nice place to relax, as the walk around Alcatraz hadn't been a leisurely stroll. Much like everywhere else in San Francisco, it seemed, there were steep hills and the misty air had nearly frozen my lungs.

We returned to the hostel, collected our things and checked out, then we checked into a different hotel, one of Luca's choosing.

The Loews Regency Bridge to Bridge suite was more in keeping with Donato expectations. The view from the private terrace was stunning with the Bay and Golden Gate Bridges both visible on good days. I tried not to sigh with relief at the sumptuous king-size bed dominating the room, but my bones were eager to sleep in all that luxury after suffering through a night in the hostel bed.

I'd almost forgotten how nice Luca could be. Whereas some people with obscene wealth were wretched to servers, Luca was different. Although firm, he always treated them, from the housekeepers to the valet, with respect, and he believed in rewarding those who performed well.

I had to admit, it was a tiny notch in his favor. I abhorred assholes who treated other people as beneath them.

After tipping the bellhop, he closed the door and immediately started making calls, all the while instructing me to enjoy a bath while he handled some business before our dinner tonight.

"I thought we were going shopping," I said.

He paused in his call to say, "Clothes will be delivered within the hour. By the time you're finished, you'll have clothes to wear to dinner."

Of course. I bit back a sigh. I could only imagine what would be awaiting me when I finished my bath. I didn't like the feeling of being dressed up like a doll, but he was already in business mode and anything I said would be a waste of energy.

Besides, it was only for a short time. No matter what

he had in store for me tonight, nothing would change my mind.

The fact was, even if I was in love with Luca—which I wasn't—I would never stay.

The fear that I couldn't go through with the wedding had started six months ago. I couldn't shake the horrible feeling that I'd be walking down the aisle toward someone I didn't trust.

I wasn't hardwired for a business-type marriage. I wanted the real deal, the love and butterflies, the romance.

If we chose to have children, I wanted those children conceived in love, not obligation.

Luca's mother had already started talking about the appropriate timeline for her first grandchild, which had really put me off.

Maybe I didn't want to get pregnant on her social schedule. Maybe I didn't want to have kids at all—I didn't know—but I did know that someone else wasn't going to be in charge of my fallopian tubes.

Luca was expected to take over the family business once Giovanni retired, but seeing as the old grump seemed to sip on the spring water of eternal life, I suspected he'd outlive us all, which meant we'd never escape his influence.

Much like the Donato boys, I'd been raised by a nanny, but from the time I was thirteen, I was invited to the Donato mansion for their social events, which were frequent, so sometimes I felt I knew the Donato home better than my own. Once I turned sixteen, I was invited to private dinners so I could get to know my future husband under the watchful eyes of our parents.

It's amazing what kids can adjust to.

I'm not sure if it was a tragedy or a blessing that I'd fallen in love with Luca on my own.

I sank into the bath, blissing out in the luxury of the massive sunken tub as the jets pulsated beneath my sore muscles.

Walking anywhere in San Francisco was like training for a triathlon, and I was sorely out of shape, if my screaming thigh muscles were any indication of my fitness level.

A short knock at the door interrupted my contented sigh. "Yes?" I asked, wondering what Luca could need.

"May I come in?"

It was stupid, but I was charmed by his courtesy. Luca made no secret that he wanted me, but thus far, we'd avoided having sex. "Y-yes," I answered, my voice catching. I cleared my throat and tried again with a clear yes.

Luca came in, shirtless, I might add, and handed me a flute of champagne—my favorite drink—along with a small tray of chocolate-dipped strawberries.

I grinned, not bothering to hide my excitement at the welcome snack. We hadn't eaten since brunch. He placed the tray next to me and went to the sink to rinse the sweat of the day from his face. My belly tingled as I toyed with an outrageous offer, knowing it was a bad idea, but the allure of danger had always been my downfall.

"If you want to join me, you can," I offered politely. I mean, he had brought me delicious goodies, and it seemed only fair to share the tub before dinner so he could use the jets on his muscles, too. Between last night's awful sleep and then walking around all day, he must be suffering as much as I was.

"You sure?" Luca asked with an uncertain smile that was both endearing and sexy at the same time—*yep, dangerous.* "Aren't you afraid I'll catch an illicit eyeful of titty or I might offend you with my naked body?"

"Your body was never the problem" dropped from my mouth before I could stop it. *Damn champagne, loosening the gears on my jaw, apparently.* "Look, we can be adults. We've already seen each other naked plenty of times, but the bubbles provide a modicum of privacy and you look like you could use the jets, too."

"All right," Luca said with a nod, popping the button on his jeans with a deliberate motion that made all the nerve endings in my body wake up and take notice. I pretended to be unaffected by his seemingly unintentional strip tease and looked away just as he dropped his boxer briefs.

Luca slid into the tub, giving me the all clear with a "Your virgin eyes are safe," the laughter in his voice coaxing a smile from my lips.

His deep sigh as he sank lower into the water did terrible things to my determination, but I'd put myself in this situation, perhaps as a test. I was in a giant bubbly tub with Luca, undoubtedly the sexiest man I'd ever known.

And we were both naked.

Because we were in the tub.

Together.

If I could get through this without succumbing to

my baser desires, I was golden. I could get through the
week, no problem.

Oh, Mother Mary. My fingers itched to curl around
his cock. If he wasn't hard already, I knew it wouldn't
take long. I sank lower into the bubbles so he didn't see
my nipples pearling, ready.

I might have overestimated my own strength. My
own hubris might've just screwed me harder than Luca
ever could.

"Admit it…you hated the hostel," Luca challenged
with a teasing grin. I laughed, relieved to draw my focus
away from the pornographic thoughts populating my
brain. "C'mon, just admit it. I know you well enough
to know that, for you, sharing a bathroom with strangers was the worst thing ever."

"I didn't love it… Sort of like dorm life, " I hedged,
not quite willing to concede that my booking had been
a terrible idea, insisting that the run-down roach motel
had a "certain charm." But I couldn't sell the outright lie
with any conviction and we both knew it. I relented with
a resigned bite into another strawberry. "Okay, yes, I
hated the hostel. It was awful, but to be fair, the pictures
on the website were far more quaint and boho chic."

"You thought it was going to be like 'glamping,'" he
correctly assumed with amusement, and I both hated
and enjoyed that he knew me so well.

"Nico told me about that time you and your brothers
got the bright idea to try camping behind your house.
None of you had ever pitched a tent before, but you refused to ask for help. Nico said you nearly suffocated

when the whole thing collapsed in the middle of the night."

"That was Dante's fault. He was in charge of the poles, but he took shortcuts and I was practically brained when the top pole came down on my face. I had a black eye for a week."

"What'd you say you got the black eye from?"

"Sailboat accident," he answered with a grin. "Sounded much better than how it actually happened. Did Nico also happen to share that he was the first to run back to the house like a giant baby, leaving us in the dust? He'd thought a bear attacked the tent."

"He did not share that part," I admitted, laughing. I could believe Nico booking it back to the house, shrieking. "To be fair, he's the youngest. He was probably pretty freaked out."

"We all were," Luca said, sharing my laughter. "You try being woken out of a sound sleep by the sound of tearing nylon and poles clattering all around you. I think Dante pissed his pants."

I giggled at the vision of Dante, the smug prick, wetting himself. "I might enjoy that vision a little too much."

"You and Dante were never close," Luca said, shaking his head.

"He was always so mean."

"Probably had a crush on you. Lord knows, half the guys in your class did—Nico told me. Can't say I blame them... I felt the same way."

Luca's quiet compliment caused a strawberry to lodge in my throat for a brief second. I swallowed, meeting

his gaze, shocked, not so much by his admission but because it was the first time Luca had ever shared something so private and real with me.

Luca broke the spell, saying with a crooked grin,
"Not a bad first day in San Francisco. Bet your feet are
killing you, though."

I jerked a short nod, tangled momentarily in the complicated threads that wound around us.

Luca surprised me by finding my foot beneath the
water and gently rubbing the insole. I groaned without thought.

He shifted, murmuring, "Keep making sounds like
that and I'll start rubbing more than your feet."

I bit my lip before challenging him to go for it. I was
playing with fire, but I'd forgotten how addictive the
heat between Luca and me had always been.

When we'd been together, the sexual tension had been
off the charts. It was no different now, except everything
was different.

We weren't young lovers anymore. There were only
expectations and family drama between us now. Something Luca had mentioned earlier rose up in my memory, and it occurred to me that I'd never considered
how the pressure to live up to Giovanni's expectations
might weigh on Luca.

Neither of us had been given a choice in the way we
were raised and how we were expected to fulfill our
obligations.

"Do you love your father?" I asked.

My question took him aback. "That's an odd question," he said slowly, trying to figure out where my head was. "Do you love your father?"

"No." My answer was simple. "How can I? He's a stranger. My mother died when I was two. Instead of raising me with love within a real father-daughter relationship, he tossed me into the arms of a nanny. I was expected to be polished and pretty so that I reflected well on his image, but I was nothing but a bartering chip to him. When he and your father arranged this marriage, I'd served my only purpose. Why would I love a man like that?"

Luca nodded, a hint of shame coloring his cheeks. Did it embarrass him how I'd come into his life? I knew Luca didn't approve of his father's actions, but he'd been young, too—what choice had he had?

Both of us had been powerless to affect the situation we were put into.

But I wanted to know, did he love his father?

"Pretty deep question for a soak that's meant to be relaxing," he finally answered, his brow lifting in question. When I didn't let him off the hook, he sighed, saying, "I don't know. My relationship with my father is…what you'd call strained. But I suppose somewhere, deep down, I love him. He is my father, after all. He afforded me many opportunities, and he's taught me how to succeed in a cutthroat world. I owe him my respect, if nothing else."

"That sounds like something you'd say about an asshole mentor, not your father."

"He's a difficult man."

I suppose that was a fair answer to an unfair question.

"Let me wash your back," he suggested, changing the subject. I hesitated, but we were already in the bathtub naked together, and it'd been my idea—not sure how I could possibly try to maintain some sort of distance now. I turned around and scooted toward Luca, sliding between his legs.

The soft washcloth on my back felt good. I closed my eyes and enjoyed the simple pleasure.

Then I felt Luca's lips brush against the top of my shoulder and I shuddered with a tiny sharp inhale, the only sound between us.

"Every inch of you is perfection," he murmured, pressing another kiss to the column of my neck. I arched slightly, giving him better access, which he took without reservation. "Your taste, your smell, the way you cry out when you come. You're all I ever think about."

His hands reached around to cup my breasts possessively. There was such hunger in his touch I practically vibrated with the need to feel him inside me. There was something so arousing about the way he held me tight, his palms filled with my tits, the hardened nipples poking out between splayed fingers. He knew how responsive my nipples were. All it would take for me to lose all sense of reason would be for him to latch onto my breasts with that greedy mouth.

"We should get ready," he said against my skin, pressing one last kiss against my bare shoulder as he released me.

I fought to control the rush of disappointment. "Good idea," I agreed with false calm as I scooted away so he could climb out of the tub. This time I didn't avert my eyes. A smile curved my lips as his cock sprang out, hard and ready, from the nest of dark hair.

At least I wasn't the only one suffering.

But this was good, I told myself. Sex would only complicate an already messed-up situation, and it might contaminate my judgment. I didn't want anything to veer me off course.

Eventually, I'd forget how good we were together between the sheets.

Eventually.

CHAPTER TWELVE

Luca

DRESSED IN A sharp black suit, my shoes gleaming in the soft light, I'd just finished straightening my cuff links when the door opened and Katherine emerged. I'd been waiting for her to finish her hair and makeup, which had given me time to assemble her wardrobe choices for the night.

Fluffy white towel wrapped around her, Katherine stared, her mouth dropping at the glittering diamond accessories that accompanied each outfit choice. I wanted to ensure she had the pick of whatever style she wanted, so I'd had my assistant send samples from every designer in the city and had those matched with appropriately decadent jewelry choices.

Diamonds, rubies, emeralds, pearls, sapphires…it was an assortment of breathtaking jewels fit for a queen. The Donato name carried enough clout that I was able to get the gems on loan for the evening, likely because the jeweler hoped I would purchase at least one of the offered beauties by morning.

Katherine stood at the edge of the bed, staring down at the selections. "Are you insane? Where are we going to dinner, the Taj Mahal?"

"You'd be surprised how difficult it is to get reservations," I quipped with a small smile. She glanced up in question, her brow furrowed. "I wanted to ensure that wherever we went, you were the brightest diamond in the room."

She flushed and bit her lip, reluctantly flattered. "But, Luca... I...I don't know what to say except I can't wear any of this..." she said, even as her eyes were drawn to the brilliant sapphire drop pendant that was my personal favorite. She would look stunning in the blue dress with that pendant around her neck.

"Why not?" I asked.

"This is all too much."

"They're loaners for now, and I promise you don't have to accept any gifts you don't want. You like the sapphire?"

Her gaze returned to the gem, blinking as she swallowed. "Yes, but..."

"Then you shall wear it," I said, moving to clasp the pendant for her. It hung like a blue teardrop just above her cleavage, a promise of pleasure to come. I hardened instantly at the thought of Katherine wearing the sapphire and nothing else. My fingers itched to relieve her of the towel, but I refrained. Instead, I said, "And the dress? What do you think?"

She dragged her gaze away from the pendant, looking toward the dress. All she could do was nod, finally admitting, "It's gorgeous, too."

"Excellent." I felt the tension lift from my shoulders. "Do you need help slipping it on?" *Please say yes*, I practically begged with my eyes, but she carefully scooped up the dress and disappeared into the bathroom, closing the door behind her. I chuckled and rubbed the sudden damp from my forehead. If she liked the blue dress, wait until she saw what I had planned for dessert...

When Katherine emerged from the bathroom moments later, the deep blue of the dress clinging to her curves like a second skin, the sapphire pendant winking from her throat, I nearly buckled in an embarrassing display of total weakness.

I'd never met another woman who made me feel the way Katherine did. I was old enough to realize I never would.

With her hair swept up into a messy bun and a little makeup on, she was perfect. Katherine had a natural beauty that most women would kill for.

Frankly, I thought she was gorgeous from the moment she opened her eyes in the morning, bedhead and all, but now was not the time to share that sentiment. She was too skittish yet to hear anything so raw. When she'd been ready to hear it, I hadn't been ready to share, and now we were playing on opposite sides of the field. I suppose I was to blame, but a Donato didn't look backward. *Push forward to victory*.

Unsticking my tongue from the roof of my mouth, I offered a sincere compliment, saying, "Stunning. I'm glad you chose the blue."

She blushed, and her fingers found the pendant. "As

long as I don't get robbed at gunpoint later," she joked. "It's like wearing a giant target on my chest."

"You'll be perfectly safe," I assured her, crooking my arm for her to slip her hand into. We left the room and got into the elevator. In truth, I would tear apart with my bare hands anyone who dared to hurt Katherine. Did that threat extend to my own family? My father was a stubborn bully, but would he actually go through with ruining Katherine if I intervened? I couldn't let him do that. Defying my father wasn't high on my list of desirables, so I'd just have to make sure I didn't lose.

"Are you okay?" Katherine asked, noting the sudden tension in my body. "You have a pensive expression."

"I'm fine," I lied with an engaging smile. "Just wondering how I'm going to keep my hands to myself during dinner when I want to do unspeakably dirty things to you in that gorgeous dress."

She gasped and blushed, but this time she didn't hit me with a disapproving glare. Could it be Katherine was softening? I wasn't about to look a gift horse in the mouth, but I wasn't going to celebrate prematurely, either. We got off at the ground floor and exited the hotel.

"So where are we going for dinner?" she asked as I helped her into the waiting town car. "Although I think I'm too nervous to eat. What if I spill on this incredible dress? I'm such a klutz. What if I end up with a buttered roll between my boobs?"

"Then I would be a gentleman and fish it out." *With my mouth.* At her shy smile, I added, "You're the only woman I know who can find some way to wear her food at some point during the meal." When she started to frown, I hurried to add, "And I find it one of your more endearing qualities, believe it or not."

"I don't believe it," Katherine responded, smoothing the lines from her dress as she settled in her seat. "But you always were a smooth talker. I won't hold it against you."

"That's a plus," I said with a rueful chuckle, returning to the subject of dinner. "Tonight, we have dinner reservations in the private section at Cafe Zoetrope. I think you'll love the ambience."

At the mention of filmmaker Francis Ford Coppola's San Francisco restaurant, Katherine stilled the anxious fidgeting of her fingers on her matching clutch. I pretended not to notice how her breath had become shallow and her eyes had widened. "The actual Cafe Zoetrope?" she asked breathily.

I pretended ignorance. "You've heard of it?"

"I think I read something about it online," Katherine hedged, not willing to divulge her true pleasure at my choice. This woman would concede no easy victories. Under normal circumstances, I would enjoy the challenge, but I needed a win.

"Thank you for tonight," she said, her gaze dipping with a bashfulness that I found incredibly alluring. "You didn't have to do all this, but I appreciate the thoughtfulness."

My pride swelled. Being able to coax a smile from Katherine's supple lips was the best feeling in the world, but it made me greedy for more. I wanted to throw diamonds and whatever else she might want at her feet if it meant earning genuine happiness from her. "It suits you. The blue compliments your skin tone perfectly. You should trust me to always know what will make you shine."

The budding warmth fled from her eyes as she looked away. "I like to figure out for myself what works and what doesn't."

Damn it. My damn arrogance would be my downfall when it came to Katherine. Swallowing my pride, I said, "Of course. I'm humbled that you agreed with my choice."

She shot me a quick, rueful glance as if to say, *You? Humble?* And I wanted to admit, *Yeah, hard pill to swallow, but I'm truly trying.* However, I said nothing. I didn't trust my mouth not to fuck it up.

We arrived at Zoetrope, entering through a private door reserved for VIPs and members of the Coppola family, and were seated at a cozy table surrounded by memorabilia from Coppola's films throughout the years.

In spite of my gaffe only moments prior, Katherine was entranced with my restaurant choice.

"This is incredible," she breathed, her eyes sparkling with wonder. "I love his films and his spirit. This is a man who never gave up on his dreams and goals, no matter that to others he seemed to fail several times. I'm in awe of that kind of grit and talent. And entrepreneurship! I mean restaurant, winery, filmmaker, father…the man is an inspiration."

And I'm in awe of you.

She caught me watching her, her smile faltering before she asked, "How'd you know I would love a place like this? I've never told you about my fascination with Francis Ford Coppola."

"I pay attention to the things that matter to you," I answered. "You own every one of his movies on DVD, and you once mentioned that you wanted to take a trip to California to see his winery." Not to mention, I knew she'd recently sent her résumé to the winery's marketing department.

Her cheeks flushed a becoming shade of pink. "You remember that?"

"Of course."

It'd been a casual comment, but when she'd talked about Coppola, my jealousy had flared. I'd wanted to be the sole reason her face lit up like a Christmas tree. I'd been too young to appreciate that learning what made my woman tick was a gift, but then, I'd fully taken for granted that Katherine was mine and always would be, so I hadn't spent much effort in ensuring she was happy.

The waitstaff, impeccably trained, took our orders and left us to ourselves. The wine helped ease the tension, but I was suddenly agitated. Too many thoughts racing through my head. Too many pitfalls to stumble onto and break my neck.

Confidence had always been my strength, my armor. My fear that none of my usual tricks would work left me flailing with a flimsy strategy, and with the stakes as high as they were, I couldn't afford to make stupid mistakes.

I needed Katherine in my bed, but it had to be timed perfectly. Each time I pushed and pulled away, I drove her frustration higher so that when I finally got between her legs, she'd remember why we were so good together.

Bone-melting orgasms were going to be my secret weapon to cracking open that locked heart.

"When did your fascination with Coppola begin?" I asked, seeking safe ground.

"I don't know when it happened, exactly, but it might've started with the first time I saw *The Outsiders*."

"The movie with Matt Dillon?"

She bobbed her head. "Yep. Here's the thing, it was on late-night television, I was up studying for exams, and I put it on for background noise. But slowly I started to catch snippets of the movie, and before I knew it, I was totally engrossed and bawling my head off by the end. Something about that movie just touched my soul." She risked a short laugh. "I know that sounds corny, but the movie is pure genius, and that, of course, sparked an interest in who directed the film, and I found Coppola. The rest just seemed to flow into a genuine obsession that I can't explain, but it's my guilty pleasure."

It was the first real bit of personal information Katherine had willingly shared all week, and I was eager for more, even if I wanted to be the one who created that megawatt smile instead of an old filmmaker she'd never met.

Our food arrived—*linguine alla vongole* for me and *bumbola ai broccoli e salsiccia* for Katherine—and we enjoyed the culinary perfection of old-world Italian cooking.

"Reminds me of my great-grandmother's linguine,"

I said with a bit of nostalgia. "Nonna was a feisty thing, but, damn, she could whip up a mean table."

"That's the one who lived in Italy, right?"

I nodded. "My father's grandmother Francesca Donato. She died when I was ten, but she made sure to teach her daughters how to make fresh pasta the Italian way."

"Your nonna would've loved Greta," Katherine quipped with a knowing grin.

Our cook, Greta, ruled the Donato kitchens with an iron fist. She was the female version of my father. She believed in old-school traditions and would skin alive anyone who dared to take shortcuts when it came to what landed on the Donato table.

"That she would," I agreed. The stout Italian woman had starch flowing through her veins, but she could make your mouth orgasm with her culinary skills. If Dante kept eating Greta's pasta the way he did, he'd end up fat as a summer tick. Actually, I'd like to see that—the asshole could use something to take him down a peg. I rubbed my belly, suffering my own indulgence. Time to walk off some of this dinner, but first, "Dessert?" I asked.

"God, no." She shook her head and groaned. "I can't fit anything else in my stomach."

"Me, either." I signaled for the check, paid, and we made our way into the brisk night air. Fog had begun to settle. The pale, misty blanket cloaked the city streets with an eerie elegance, but it chilled to the bone quickly. We managed a few blocks before we hurried back to the awaiting town car, our noses tingling with the cold.

"What now?" she asked, curious as she rubbed her hands together to warm them. "We could see a movie... We could probably even find a theater showing Coppola films."

I laughed at her not-so-subtle hint. "As much as I would love sitting in a darkened theater with you, I have different plans."

"Oh? Do tell."

"It's a surprise. I recall that you used to enjoy surprises."

"I was younger then," she reminded me, her expression wary.

"True. I guess you'll just have to trust me."

My next move was a gamble. It could blow up in my face or put her in my bed. What I was about to expose Katherine to was above and beyond anything she could possibly imagine.

I didn't have the option of taking the safe route. It was go big or go home.

We returned to our hotel, and as directed, a new selection of outfits awaited Katherine.

Only this time instead of jeweled necklaces for accessories, there were ornate masquerade-style masks.

"What the hell... Where are we going?" Katherine asked, her gaze roaming the beautiful masks and their accompanying corsets of black, red and purple lace before turning to me for answers, balking openly. "I'm not wearing any of those anywhere in public."

I closed the distance between us with strong, purposeful steps until I was close enough to draw her to me. She melted in my arms even as her gaze remained cautious. I brushed my lips across hers as I murmured, "I can promise you…where we are going is very, *very* private." I released her reluctantly, her lips still dewy from my kiss. "Time to get dressed. We don't want to be late."

CHAPTER THIRTEEN

Katherine

MY HEART HAMMERED in my chest. The lingerie on the bed beckoned with wicked fingers, promising a night that would live in my dreams forever—but was I willing to allow such a memory to exist?

"No sex?" I repeated the question, my throat suddenly dry. "If I wear this…will you still stick to our agreement?"

"Darling, I've been good so far," he reminded me, and I blushed. *Yes, I am the one who's having trouble remembering our deal.* In hindsight, I should've forbidden all kissing when we struck our deal. Too late now.

"I will not fuck you until you beg for it," he returned, but his blue eyes glittered with a secret that I didn't trust and desperately needed to know. Still, I hesitated, afraid that he was going to find a way to put me on my back, in spite of our deal. Mostly afraid because I wanted him to. The tension coiling in my body was enough to crush a Smart car. I craved his touch, craved the feeling of him inside me, pushing me toward that brink of disaster, but I was trying to remain strong. As long as he kept his promise…I could get through this.

"I don't beg," I answered, my fingers trailing across the lacy texture of the black corset, the long garter straps dangling in wait. The accompanying mask was a thing of art. I perused the selections, each more beautiful than the last, but my eye was drawn to the black. I wanted to slip it over my face, to lose myself in the illusion of being someone else, if only for the night. I caught the voracious look in Luca's eyes as I teased my fingers across the fabric of my favorite corset. If anyone would beg, it would be Luca. "And what are you wearing if I'm to wear this ridiculous getup?"

"Nothing quite as beautiful."

The smart part of my brain warned that I should refuse, that wherever Luca planned to take me was a bad idea, but the other part of my brain couldn't quite resist the temptation of finding out.

Curiosity would ruin me; mystery was my Pied Piper.

"Which one should I wear?" I asked coyly, enjoying the subtle bobbing of his Adam's apple. "Do you have a preference?"

"The black," he answered, his voice rough. "The same one that you can't keep your hands from."

"You always did have excellent taste," I murmured, slowly plucking the lingerie from the bed and clutching it to my chest as I headed to the bathroom. "I guess you'd better get changed, then," I said before closing the door behind me.

Was I doing this? Even though I knew it was a bad idea? That I would likely end up with Luca's cock inside me? I shivered, trying not to buckle at the sheer plea-sure of that thought. How could I miss him so much and yet hate him, too?

You don't hate Luca, a voice whispered. *You're still in love with him.*

Stunned, I rejected the silver-tongued devil in my head and carefully removed the exquisite designer dress to change into the equally gorgeous lingerie. The steel-boned corset accentuated my waist, flaring my hips, pushing my breasts up like an offering, my nipples barely covered. In fact, the dusky rose of my areolae flirted with the edge of the lace trim purposefully. One slip and my nipples would pop free, hard and pearled for Luca's hungry mouth. I caught my breath, my fin-gers shaking as I snapped the sheer garters into place. I pulled out the pins holding my hair in place. Waves tumbled to my shoulders, and I fitted the mask to my face. My lips, red as sin, pouted and promised ruin. This was insane. I was in dangerous territory, but the secret thrill at my image in the mirror was far more powerful than any voice of reason.

Drawing a deep breath, I opened the door and found Luca waiting. He'd changed into sleek, soft leather pants that on anyone else would've looked corny and trying too hard, but on Luca they looked absolutely sinful.

His shirt, casually sexy, was slightly open, hinting at the hard, muscled chest hiding beneath. My own breath hitched in my chest as warmth flooded my pelvis. If he slipped a finger inside me, he'd find me wet and ready.

"You're fucking gorgeous," Luca muttered, almost as if he were angry, but I knew it was simply raw, primal lust that roughened his tone. I knew without needing to touch that he was rock hard. I could practically feel the sexual pulse between us like a desperate heartbeat. His searing gaze left scorch marks on my soul. "Shall we?"

He produced a long, elegant trench coat for me, slipping it over my shoulders before clasping my hand in his and leading me from the room to the car.

My gaze kept drifting to Luca in question. The mystery of our destination was more than I could stand, but I savored the torture.

We pulled into a dark alley and exited the car. I remained close to Luca, the area looking sketchy as hell. He knocked on a door that I hadn't even realized was there, and a small panel opened as two eyes peered out. "Password" was all the voice said.

"Bacchanal," Luca answered calmly, and the peephole shut with a rusty click as the door opened, revealing a hulking man with a bulbous nose and a mean-eyed squint, but he stepped aside so we could pass.

We traveled a long hallway until we turned a corner, revealing the most incredible view I'd ever seen—a private world of tits and ass, throbbing music and open sexual acts happening in full view of anyone who cared to watch.

"What is this place?" I asked in shock, my gaze riveted to this buffet of sensuality.

"Welcome to Malvagio, my love," he answered with a broad grin. "Where anything goes as long as it's consensual."

"This is a…sex club?" I managed, still staring, my gaze snagging on a woman on her knees sucking a man's cock as if her life depended on the come jetting down her throat. She was naked, aside from the tiny pasties attached to her nipples and the thong that barely covered her pussy. I should've been horrified. Disgusted, even.

But I wasn't.

There was something intoxicatingly exciting about the taboo place. Everywhere I looked there was something illicit and forbidden happening right before my eyes.

After spending my life under the shadow of who I was supposed to become…the idea of being whoever I wanted within these walls had my heart hammering with instant arousal.

Damn Luca for knowing my secret perverted heart.

Luca graced me with an inquiring look as if to ask, *Shall we stay?* and I gave him a small nod and tremulous smile in answer.

The sensual energy in the club twisted a knot around my senses as we wound our way through the crowded dance floor to a raised section where a table awaited us. Luca seemed comfortable, familiar even, with the place, and I immediately had questions I shouldn't ask.

The puffed burgundy leather booth was grotesquely ornate, ostentatious and borderline in poor taste, but that was what made it perfect for the surroundings. Everything bore a decadent yet used quality that spoke of the hedonism found in this place. I couldn't stop staring, my breath suspiciously shallow, as I was bombarded with sights and sounds that were usually reserved for private moments.

A tall, broad-shouldered, dark-haired man with a curvy woman on his arm approached with a knowing grin. "Fucking Luca Donato, you son of a bitch, you came after all." He clasped Luca's hand and pumped it vigorously before they embraced in a man hug.

"Dillon Buchanan," Luca returned with an equal smirk before turning to the curvaceous woman with a respectful bow. "And you must be the woman who made an honest man out of this asshole."

Dillon beamed, making introductions. "My beautiful wife and business partner, Penny. Penny, this is Luca Donato. We used to run together back in the day."

"I won't hold that against you," Penny promised with a sweet smile before turning to me. "And you are…?"

Luca answered before I could. "My fiancée, Katherine," he said.

I quickly followed with "Pleasure to meet you," before shooting Luca an uncertain look. It was obvious Luca and Dillon knew each other from connections I had no access to. I had so many questions, but now was not the time to ask, and besides, they seemed very nice, in spite of the surroundings and the fact that I could almost see the woman's nipples overflowing from her tight bustier. I shifted a little, knowing my nipples were similarly in the danger zone of popping out.

Well, when in Rome, I guess.

"Pleased to meet you," Penny said, looping her arm around her husband. "Are you here for the auction?"

"The auction?" I repeated, confused. "What is that?"

"Darling, don't ruin the surprise," Dillon admonished when he realized I was clueless. To Luca he said,

"I'll have some champagne sent over. If you need anything, don't hesitate to drop my name."

The Buchanan couple left us, and I immediately turned to Luca. "What the hell is the auction? You're crazy if you think you're selling me to the highest bidder in this place."

He laughed as if my fear was absurd. "You should know by now I don't share."

I relaxed a little. "So, what is it, then?"

"Malvagio is very exclusive, very difficult to get into. Prospective members must earn a sponsor. Tonight, the hopefuls will step on the stage in the attempt to snag someone's interest. It's quite entertaining. I didn't know the auction was tonight when I called Dillon, but I think you'll find it worth a watch."

An auction where people hoped to be bought. What a foreign concept. I'd been bartered in a business transaction before I'd understood the meaning of the word, and yet the people here *wanted* to be bought.

Luca sensed my disquiet and leaned over to whisper in my ear, "Darling, it's all a game. A consensual game where the ultrarich get to pretend and forget their obligations for a night. No one is truly bought and sold." I relaxed until he amended his statement, saying, "Actually, that's not entirely true. Once a sponsor makes a purchase, that person is obligated to please their sponsor in any way they choose for a year. It's all in good fun, though. No one is asked to do anything against their will or comfort level."

It all sounded reasonable, except I imagined that their comfort level and mine were vastly different.

"Have you ever...sponsored someone?" I asked, though I didn't know why it mattered.

"No." I couldn't hide the whoosh of air released from my lungs, and he laughed. "Aw, if I didn't know better, I'd say my woman is a bit jealous."

"Don't flatter yourself," I replied, but the burn in my chest at the idea of Luca pleasuring anyone aside from me was telling. It also ignited a memory I'd rather forget. I settled against the plush cushions. "So, what now?"

"Now we wait for the show to begin." The champagne arrived, and he handed me a glass. "How about a toast?"

I raised my glass. "What shall we toast?"

"New beginnings?" he suggested with a cheeky grin, which I immediately countered with a brief smile.

"Closure."

The glitter in his eyes told me he wasn't pleased, but I didn't care.

I would prove to Luca that it would take more than our sexual chemistry to make me forget why I needed out of my contract.

But as I sipped my champagne, the bubbles tickling my nose, my masked gaze watching the people on the floor writhe and move to the music, a strange exhilaration loosened my inhibitions.

Tonight, hiding behind my mask, I was free to do as I pleased.

Perhaps that even meant allowing myself to have sex with Luca, one last time.

Maybe.

CHAPTER FOURTEEN

Luca

THE LIGHTS DIMMED and the crowd roared as a voice over the loudspeaker announced the beginning of the auction. All eyes went to the stage as the thick velvet curtains rose, and one after the other, the hopefuls walked the stage, the announcer listing their attributes.

"Carli is a sweet girl from a good, upstanding family in Rhode Island, but when she's not volunteering to help orphaned animals, she's taking it up the ass! That's right, Carli loves a fat cock up her ass. Who would like to plug this lovely beauty tonight? The bidding starts at ten thousand!"

Katherine giggled and clapped her hand over her mouth in delighted shock. "I can't believe this is happening. Do they write their own stuff or is this just made up?"

I shrugged. "Who knows? All I know is that just as her real name isn't Carli, I doubt any of these people do any volunteer work. Malvagio is all about satisfying the most jaded of appetites, if you know what I mean."

Katherine nodded and her eyes sparkled as she watched the carnal show. One after the other, women, all impeccably groomed and fanatically physically perfect, walked the catwalk, their talents shared with the potential sponsors.

Once the sponsor made the purchase, a golden collar was clasped around their necks, then they were led off the stage by a thin gold chain to do whatever they were asked to do.

By the end, our bottle of champagne was gone and Katherine was itching to dance.

I laughed as she grabbed my hand and dragged me to the dance floor.

Closing her eyes, she lost herself to the beat of the music, her hips swaying and grinding, a visual that nearly had me busting a nut right there on the floor.

God, she was hot.

Appreciative, and some downright hungry, glances were thrown Katherine's way, but she was oblivious, which worked in my favor, because that meant she also didn't catch the *back the fuck off* vibe I was sending to the wolves in the den.

Katherine looped her arms around me, each part of her body a perfect fit with mine, and I knew she felt the erection in my pants, but she simply laughed—the sound like gasoline on my raging libido. "Is that a banana in your pocket or are you just happy to see me?"

My strained chuckle was my only answer as I ground against her. I wanted to bury myself inside that sweet pussy—that wet haven I wanted all to myself. The restraint it took not to drag her to a darkened corner was almost more than I could bear.

But when she reached down to cup my shaft through the leather, my knees threatened to collapse. "What are you doing?" I asked, hardening even more, if that was even possible. I feared my skin would split in two at this rate.

"Probably what I shouldn't." She lifted on her tiptoes to kiss me, her tongue darting against my lips, teasing. "But then, you know that."

I whirled her around so that her ass was against my cock, holding her in place by a firm hand on her belly. Against the column of her exposed neck, I murmured, "Careful, baby girl. You're playing with fire."

"I know you want to fuck me," she dared, pushing my buttons. "And I know you think you're going to seduce me into leaving with you at the end of the week."

"And if I did?"

"Then you'd be wrong," she said, but when I surged against her, she gasped. Still, she managed with a certain "Even if I slept with you against my better judgment, breaking my own rules...it wouldn't matter. I'm not going home with you."

I growled, tightening my grip on her. "Then why tease me like this?"

"Because I miss the feel of you inside me," she admitted breathlessly, and that was all I needed. She thought it would be so easy to fuck me and walk away? She'd obviously forgotten how electric our chemistry was. *Well, guess it's time to remind her.*

Her hand in mine, I pulled her away from the dance

floor, up the stairs and down the hall to the private rooms. The doors were coded, and I knew the Buchanan men had a private room that only they were allowed to access.

I also knew their code.

Bypassing the dungeons designed for those who enjoyed BDSM, I went straight to the Buchanan suite and punched in the code, knowing ahead of time that the suite would be empty and available.

We were seconds across the threshold with the door locked behind us when I hoisted her into my arms and her legs wound around my waist as if they belonged there.

Feverish to taste and touch, we were both out of control. The burgundy walls, black decor and giant bed in the center of the room were a blur as we stumbled out of our clothes. Her soft skin, etched by the boning of the corset, trembled beneath my fingertips as I laid her on the black satin bedding.

Her hair fanned out, long, wild tendrils that begged to wrap around my hand. I reached for her mask, but she stopped me. "Leave it," she said, and I nodded. I would eagerly agree to anything she wanted tonight. I was so desperate to taste her again, to feel her close around my cock, to hear her moan my name as she came.

I slid the thong from her thighs and tossed it away. Her sweet pussy, tantalizingly bare, beckoned with a dewed slit. I licked my bottom lip, nearly insane with need. My heart almost stopped when she slowly opened her legs for me, inviting me in, spreading herself like an offering.

It was like a fevered fantasy materializing before my eyes. I knew her body so well, from the location of each mole or freckle to the delicate folds that hid her bashful clit.

"Jesus," I breathed, taking a moment to simply stare at the woman who'd become everything to me. Fuck everything else in life. I trembled with the urgency to taste her, to know her again. I wanted to sear the unique flavor of her into my brain so that all I had to do was close my eyes and be right back in this moment, my face between her thighs.

A moan escaped my lips as I nibbled that sweet, swollen nub. Tiny pulses beneath my tongue danced in time with her gasps, drawn breaths and keening cries.

"Luca!" she groaned as my tongue played and teased, my fingers sliding into her honeyed pussy as she dripped with need. I lapped at her sweetness, the musky feminine scent driving me into a raw, primal state where only one thing mattered—Katherine.

I wanted to taste every inch of her. I wanted to know how she'd changed, how she'd remained the same.

I'd introduced her to pleasure, but years had passed since that time in our lives. I was eager to show her the difference between a foolish young man and a man who'd learned the importance of patience and timing.

I wanted her to moan my name until the ringing echo of the pleasure I could give her obliterated the memory of anyone else.

Maybe I didn't have the right to believe she would always be mine—that I'd taken something so precious for granted—but when it came to Katherine, I wasn't interested in playing fair or following society's rules.

Pushing her to the edge of climax, just when I knew she was about to come, I slowed my attention and her tiny groans of desperation made me smile against her damp flesh. "So greedy," I murmured, relishing the way her body spasmed and her legs quivered. As soon as she caught her breath, I started again, slipping a finger deep inside, strumming her G-spot.

"*Oh*, God," she gasped, arching, her fingers digging into the bedding. "I can't… I can't handle it…" she pleaded, sucking air, her beautiful breasts heaving, nipples tightening. "Luca!" And then she gushed in my mouth, shattering completely.

I lapped at her, in carnal heaven. I could have buried my face between her folds and died a happy man, but I was greedy for so much more.

I climbed her body, pausing to suck a taut nipple before moving to her mouth. I wanted her to taste herself on my tongue, the unique flavor that drove me insane with need and want.

She groaned, clutching at me as I plunged my tongue into her mouth. "You taste that, baby?" I grinned against her mouth as she gasped. "That's all you, and it's hot as fuck. I love the way you taste, woman."

I swallowed the small whimpers coming from her open mouth as she recovered, her thighs splayed open as I maneuvered myself to her opening. I delved into the small bowl of complimentary condoms, sending foil packets bouncing to the floor as I fished for one. I sheathed myself with shaking fingers and then slowly fed my shaft into her slick opening.

She clasped around me like an oiled glove. My eyes rolled back as a groan escaped my slack mouth. Raw heat enveloped my cock, searing my nerve endings with intense pleasure.

Katherine clutched at me, her legs locking around my waist, driving me deeper.

"I'll never get enough of you, Katherine," I said, my voice strained as I railed her without control. She drove me insane. The suave lover had left the building and in his place was a rutting beast, but Katherine took each thrust with wild abandon, crying out, urging me on.

"Yes, Luca!" she moaned, arching against me, squeezing me from the inside, milking my cock for every drop I could possibly give her.

I couldn't hold back any longer. I wanted to last, I wanted to wow her with my sexual prowess, but I was simply out of my head with the need to reclaim what had once been mine.

I came with a shout, my hips thrusting on autopilot as I emptied myself, jet after jet. If only that fucking thin piece of latex weren't between us. I wanted her dripping with my come. I wanted to watch as it slid from her core and dribbled down her legs, so I could slip my fingers inside her, knowing I'd filled her completely.

Primal, territorial pride suffused my chest as I continued to thrust against her even as I was beginning to soften. Her tiny whimpers were like embers landing on tinder, igniting fresh sparks.

I could spend my life buried inside her, fucking her

until we were old and gray and prone to breaking a hip if we fucked too hard.

"Luca." She breathed my name, soft and fluttery as butterfly wings. My breathing harsh, I held her tight, afraid to let go. Being inside her again, feeling her clench around me—I knew if I couldn't make this work between us, I'd never feel this way again.

There was no one but Katherine for me. I wanted to tell her—to bare my soul in a way I'd never tried—but the words were stuck in my throat.

Maybe if I told her what a jackass I'd been to dick around the one person who'd known me best, the one person who'd loved me unconditionally, she might see fit to forgive me. No more manipulations or carefully thought-out seductions for the sake of winning. Just me and her, naked, rediscovering one another as lovers should.

Just do it. Open your mouth and say the words she needs to hear.

But I couldn't. I was pussing out.

Ah, hell. Katherine needed to learn to move on from the past, right? I would give her the world if she'd let me…but I couldn't fucking apologize for something that had never actually happened.

Yeah, the thing was, I'd never cheated on her, but I was guilty of something else.

When that pictured had blown everything up—I'd been relieved.

We were too young, and everything was happening too fast.

I knew Katherine had fallen hard for me, and I was

getting there, too. But Katherine still had college to get through, and I never wanted her to regret marrying me too young.

So I'd been fucking relieved when I'd inadvertently blown everything to shit with one stupid decision.

I thought with time we'd laugh about it, maybe even joke on our wedding night about how young and stupid we'd been.

I never expected our breakup to be the catalyst that propelled Katherine right into the decision that she was through with everything associated with our lives before that moment.

Including our engagement.

CHAPTER FIFTEEN

Katherine

TINY PULSES ECHOED in my body, every nerve ending alive. The satin beneath my skin, the scent of our lovemaking—everything seemed more intense, more vibrant.

How could I ever hope to be free of Luca when I knew I would forever be addicted to this feeling? Luca was in my soul, marked from the moment I gave myself to him at eighteen.

Malvagio was the epitome of sin and ruin wrapped elegantly in luxury, drugging me with its promise of secrets and anonymity. Nobody would know what we'd done here, on this bed, except me and him.

The freedom to breathe for the first time in months overrode the faint voice of reason, telling me to stop whatever was happening between us before it became a runaway train.

I pulled off my mask, my heart still fluttering like a butterfly on meth. When I finally could talk without sounding Marilyn Monroe breathless, I asked with a curious yet sated smile, "Why did you bring me here?"

I didn't regret what'd happened, even though I'd sworn on a thousand Bibles it wouldn't. A part of me had desperately wanted to be in Luca's arms. No matter what it would cost me. Therein was the crux of the issue. What I was trying to escape wasn't so much Luca, but myself. How could I respect myself if I sacrificed my will and dignity just because I couldn't end this ridiculous obsession with Luca Donato? The answer was simple—I couldn't. "Seems a lot of effort to go to just to have sex."

"Sex with you is never too much effort."

I shivered at the sensual caress of his answer.

"What if I told you that I wanted you to experience something dangerous yet safe, something that you would never forget no matter where life took you from this moment? I wanted you to be free to experience something unique, something only I could provide for you."

My breath caught as I searched his gaze. As if I could ever forget.

Who was I kidding? The writing had been on the wall from the moment I agreed to his deal. Maybe a part of me had always known, as well. "You always knew you would get me into bed. Your confidence never wavered. Why does it matter to you so much?"

"Because you're mine and you always will be."

I think the words came out of his mouth before he realized they were coming. Maybe it was on his mind and he'd just lost the ability to hold them back, but the effect was a punch to the face for both of us.

"I don't belong to anyone, least of all you." I started

to leave the bed, but he grabbed my arm and pulled me back, unwilling to let me leave without saying his piece.

"That's not what I meant. If you want me to say that I'm unhappy you were chosen as my future wife, I would be lying. You have always and will forever be the one that I want."

My breath hitched in my chest as an unwelcome emotion crowded my reason. "Why?" I asked, even though I didn't want to hear his reasons for fear of falling all over again for the man I needed to run from.

"Why does there have to be a reason? Why does there have to be a logical explanation? You, of all people, should understand that sometimes emotion and feeling do not correspond with logic and reason. It's true I could have my pick of any woman in society—there are plenty of well-heeled women who would not only throw their daughters at me but also pin their hopes on landing a Donato in some fashion—but I'm not interested in them."

How many times had I hoped and wished to hear those very words from Luca when I was hopelessly in love with him? When I'd been that starry-eyed girl believing everything that came out of his mouth. But he'd shown me that words were easy, actions were hard.

"Luca, you have always been very eloquent with your words. Doesn't mean I believe them. Not anymore. Have you forgotten? I know you better than anyone."

He surprised me with a firm shake of his head. "No, you *knew* me. The person you remember was a foolish boy who didn't understand the value of things or people. I'm not that person anymore, but you're determined to keep stuffing me into that tiny box for *your* comfort level. If you gave me the chance, I could show you that I've changed."

I regarded him intently—questions racing—while digesting his statement. Was I being foolish and narrowminded by refusing to let Luca in a second time? The stakes were so much higher now. I wasn't just risking a broken heart; I was risking my future. Once I took those vows, I would never be able to walk away from the Donato family. *Ever.* They didn't believe in divorce. It was death do us part.

"I want to marry you, Katherine," he said, breaking into my thoughts. "I want to pledge my life to you and give you everything you deserve. All you want to do is run without even giving me a chance."

"I did give you a chance—you ruined it."

Luca's grunt of frustration grated on my nerves. I wasn't the one being difficult.

"Stop living in the fucking past. I told you, I was a kid. I wasn't ready to settle down and I hurt you. All I can say is I'm sorry."

"So you're saying now you're ready to be a faithful partner?" I didn't buy it. He could talk all he wanted and fill my head with pretty lies, but it wouldn't change the truth. Donatos followed their own code of conduct, and it was biased toward the family. They did not bend to the will of another person, and they did not take other people's feelings into consideration. "Luca, there's a reason the Donato family has managed to carve a permanent place in the top echelon of society. I'm not stupid, and I'm not blind. I know the Donato family is feared *and* respected. I also know that I don't want to be part of that anymore."

Luca looked as if he wanted to shake my head from my shoulders. I could understand his frustration, as he wasn't used to being denied, but I would never be the wife he wanted.

"Jesus, Katherine," he muttered, shoving his hand through his hair. "Why is it always the same damn argument?"

"Because you never listen to me," I returned, folding my arms. "Trust me, I'm doing you a favor."

"How so?" he asked, as if humoring me.

I tried not to bare my teeth at his condescension. "I will never be the subservient, doting wife who walks two steps behind you and defers to your judgment in any and all things like some modern-day geisha."

"I never said I wanted that!"

I startled at his sudden shout.

His nostrils flared as he cast me a dark look, but I wasn't backing down.

"That's how your entire family works," I said. "You've been raised to take over the Donato family empire. How can I know for sure you'll be any different? There's an expectation, and I have no interest in fulfilling the role of your wife under those conditions."

"And what if I said screw the traditions? I just want you. I want you in whatever way that you would be willing to have me."

My mouth opened in surprise. Was that a hint of desperation in his voice? Couldn't be. Luca was always in control, always pulling the strings behind the scenes.

Luca took my silence as an opportunity to jump in. "Let me show you the man I can be. Let me show you how it can be between us. All I want is you by my side, and if that means bucking tradition and forging a new way for the Donato family, I am willing to do that. But you have to be willing to give me a chance."

Everything he said was true. I was afraid of giving him the chance to prove me wrong. If I admitted that he had changed and that there was a possibility that he and I could actually ride off into the sunset, happy, just like I'd always hoped and dreamed, it would mean taking a chance on an unknown future where anything could happen—both good and bad. Luca had the power to destroy me completely. I was afraid of taking a chance, of giving him the keys to my happiness.

But a part of me desperately wanted to run straight to his arms, close my eyes and allow everything that Luca was envelop me. I knew it was a contradiction, but when I was with Luca, I felt safe. In those moments, I knew that Luca would never let anything happen to me, that he would destroy anyone or anything who threatened me. The irony was that he was the one who had hurt me in the first place.

I should have stuck to my guns and just kept him at a distance. Sex clouded judgment. My body still echoed with his touch—I could smell him on my skin.

"Luca, if I were to give you the opportunity to show me how different you are, what would we do?" I asked, unsure. I was walking on an iced lake, each step a gamble, but a part of me wanted to believe in the fairy tale, if only for tonight.

"Anything you want," he answered without a hint of artifice or manipulation.

Fear and uncertainty fought a battle with hope and longing. Was I willing to see Luca differently? Was I willing to put my heart on the line for a second time when the stakes were so fucking high?

"Say yes," he urged, my entire future riding on one seemingly small choice. "Say yes, Katherine. *Please*."

"I'm afraid," I whispered. "What if you hurt me again?"

"I won't."

"You don't know that."

"Let me show you."

Luca held my gaze as we both held our breath. The energy in the room swirled with possibility. I swallowed. My brain knew the right way to respond, but my lips were moving before conscious thought could stop them.

"Okay, Luca…"

And it was done.

Brain, zero. Heart, one.

CHAPTER SIXTEEN

Luca

I IGNORED THE pinch of guilt as I gathered Katherine into my arms, squeezing tight. I had broken through the first barrier. Someday she would realize that this had been the right choice.

"Thank you," I murmured against the crown of her head, inhaling the citrus scent of her hair. "I will show you that I'm a different man."

That part wasn't a lie. I wasn't the same kid who had carelessly broken her heart without realizing the depth of his consequences.

Of course, in some ways that was a good thing and in some ways it wasn't. I knew the value of having solid people in your corner, but I also knew that you couldn't always afford honesty.

But for now, we were cocooned in Malvagio's nest of iniquity, safe from prying eyes and free to be whomever we chose.

And in this moment, I chose to be her willing everything.

I rose and poured cold artisan water into frosted glasses for us both. She accepted the water and finished it with greedy gulps and a satisfied sigh. "Perfect," she murmured with a smile as I agreed.

Once finished, I climbed back into the bed and pulled her close. I would worship her body many times tonight, but for now I was content to just hold her.

Her arms closed around me as her head nestled on my chest.

"Tell me about this place," she said with a small giggle. "I mean, a sex club operating right under the nose of the snootiest people in society? I would kill to see the looks on some of those snobby matrons if they found out who exactly was a member."

I tapped her nose playfully. "That's the point—they never will. Malvagio's member list is a closely guarded secret. That's why it's so difficult to get a sponsor and even more so to become a member."

"So what's the point? All this cloak-and-dagger, secret passwords, anonymity…it's kinda silly, don't you think?"

"Of course it is, but as you know, the wealthy bore easily. Malvagio plays to their twisted sense of privilege, and the Buchanans were brilliant enough to take advantage."

"How do you know the Buchanans?"

"Dillon and I met in grad school. Jesus, he was crazy. I never saw a man treat his body the way he did and not die as a consequence. But he dropped out of grad school before getting his degree—something about his old man cutting him off. We lost touch until a few years later, when I saw him by chance in a bar, still abusing his liver with impunity, but he'd changed from a reckless asshole to a ruthless prick who'd amassed quite a fortune on his own, without his daddy's money. I was fucking impressed."

"That is impressive," Katherine agreed.

"I was happy for him. His dad...what a piece of work. You think my father is an overbearing dick? Dillon's father made my father look like Santa Claus."

Katherine looked up at me. "Seriously? That's pretty bad."

"Yeah, the Buchanans got all messed up. Honestly, I don't even know how Dillon managed to find a woman like Penny to straighten him out. All the Buchanan boys have changed for the better, but damn, I never would've thought it could happen."

Katherine cast a dubious glance my way, saying, "Well, they do own a clandestine sex club—they can't be all that lily-white and reformed."

I laughed. "True enough. I guess they were lucky enough to find accommodating women."

"I guess so."

She traced a small circle around my nipple, causing it to perk immediately. I sucked in a tight breath. "Careful, or you're going to get fucked again."

"I'm not complaining," she answered coyly. "If there's one thing you do well, it's what you do in bed."

"Perhaps I should put it on my résumé."

"Perhaps."

I resisted the urge to push at my growing erection. Any touch would only make things worse. I tried to focus. Clearing my throat, I said, "The club was actually started by Nolan and Vince, Dillon's twin brothers. Dillon only just recently acquired the club when Nolan decided he no longer wanted to be in the sex club business. Actually, it was his wife that suggested he find someone else to run the club, and he was eager to make her happy."

"You mean his wife didn't like her husband running a sex club? Go figure," she said, chuckling.

"The Buchanan boys are the most wild, lecherous, fun-loving perverts I've ever known in my life. But once they got married, they became downright respectable. A little boring, if you ask me."

"So you think marriage makes men boring?"

I answered her no doubt calculated question carefully.

"No, I think *they* got boring. I think that if you and I were married, there wouldn't be a boring day for the rest of our lives."

That part was true. I didn't doubt that there would always be sparks and fireworks between Katherine and me. Our chemistry couldn't be faked. There were some people in your life who interconnected with your soul in a way that was rare and precious. I wasn't saying that the Buchanan men hadn't found that—hell, maybe they had—all I knew was that I saw no reason to give up a harmless hobby just because another person said so.

"How long have you been coming to Malvagio?" she asked.

"Over the years, a handful of times. It isn't one of those places where you want to spend too much of your time. It's like eating a finely crafted dessert—too much of it is just too much."

"Have you ever bought someone at the auction?"

"No."

"Why not?"

I chuckled. "Because as much as I enjoy Malvagio, I'm not interested in sponsoring someone into the club. It takes too much time and effort. You have to understand most of the people who frequent this place are trust-fund babies who wouldn't understand the concept of working for a living. I don't have that problem. Boredom has never been my issue. I'm running the Donato empire, so free time isn't something I have too much of."

I enjoyed my captive audience. For the first time in years, Katherine was actually listening.

"And, to be honest," I added with a shrug, "it's fun and games when you're drunk and everyone's naked and fucking, but by the light of day, it's like the mornings at a strip club—sad, run-down and smelling of stale beer and bad decisions."

"This is the nicest strip club I've ever seen," she joked. "But I get what you're saying. It is a little on the sleazy side, but in an intoxicating way. As in, you know it's bad, but you want it anyway."

I laughed. "Dillon will be happy to hear his branding is hitting the mark. That's exactly how it's supposed to be. He doesn't want people trying to live here. It's a place where people can indulge their fantasies, have fun in a safe environment and leave in the morning with a secret. That's pretty much it. And because they don't need the income, the money that the club makes actually goes to help fund a women's shelter."

Katherine lifted her head to peer at me with questions. "What do you mean?"

It wasn't common knowledge, as the Buchanans liked to keep their business private, but sharing this information with Katherine would go a long way toward showing her that I wanted to be different.

"A handful of years ago, someone gained access to one of the Malvagio dungeons and nearly killed a woman named Lana Winters. Lana's sister, Emma, came to Malvagio with the intent of exposing the club but ended up a victim of the same person who'd assaulted her sister. Vince tried to save the club by helping Emma, and they ended up falling in love."

"That's some love story," Katherine said wryly. "And by help...you mean..."

"Oh, Vince totally kidnapped her to keep her from going to the police, but he made sure she had the best care while she recovered."

"He *kidnapped* her?"

The story was not your typical meet-cute, but nothing the Buchanans did was ever by the book. I'd learned to just go with it. "But they fell in love eventually," I reminded Katherine, adding when she gasped in feminine outrage, "And the incident left an impact on the Buchanan brothers. So they wanted to make sure that even though Malvagio might look like Sodom and Gomorrah at its finest, at the end of the day all proceeds go to help various nonprofit organizations, which are routed through the Buchanan trust, so as not to embarrass anyone."

Katherine lost some of her ire. "I guess that's admirable. What kind of donations are we talking about?"

I laughed. "Let's just say it's more than enough to keep the nonprofits comfortable and doing their good work."

"I guess that's one way to keep the balance," she supposed, pausing to straddle me. Katherine regarded me with an arched brow, her hair tumbling around her shoulders. "And how many women have you fucked in this place, Luca?"

It was a loaded question. "You know there's a law about self-incrimination," I teased, reaching up to tweak her rose-hued nipple. "Surely you aren't asking me to divulge information that might make me look like an asshole when things were going so nicely between us."

"Withholding information doesn't make the truth any less of what it is," she said.

I anchored my hands at her waist, loving the feel of her hips beneath my fingertips. "Are you sure you want me to answer?"

"I wouldn't have asked if I didn't want to know. I have no illusions that you've been celibate all these years, Luca. For that matter, I haven't been, either."

My fingers tightened. Her smile told me she knew exactly what she was doing.

I surged against her, impatient to claim her again, no matter how many men she'd been with. "You really want to know?"

"I do."

"I don't know the number. I never kept track. But I will tell you this," I said, rolling her to her back, rising above her. "You're the only one that matters."

Sealing my mouth to hers, I silenced any further questions about past lovers. I didn't want to know about hers, and I certainly didn't want to share about mine.

I'd been with scores of women across the globe, from wild to mild, but I'd never found a woman who ignited everything inside me the way Katherine did.

In some ways Dante was right—my brother had always maintained that Katherine was not a good fit as my wife. She would never be malleable or dutiful, content to be arm candy, happy to serve my every need. *Thank God.*

I wanted exactly what Katherine was—the exact opposite of whomever Dante and my father thought I should marry.

I kissed her hard and deep, the thoughts in my head crowding the lust in my heart. I didn't want to think about strategy, even though I should.

In truth, if I had never hurt her, she wouldn't have grown.

I know, I was a bastard for saying it, but it was no less true.

If I'd never broken her heart, she wouldn't have been forced to be the woman she was now, the woman capable of standing beside me. The one who would fight with and fight for me—but I couldn't say this to her without sounding like the arrogant ass she already believed I was.

Private epiphanies were best felt by the heart, not forced down your throat.

"You're so damn beautiful," I whispered, my lips blazing a trail down her silky skin, returning to her soft mouth. I drank in her breath as she groaned, our bodies pressed against each other.

"Luca," she moaned as I dragged my mouth down to her molten core. I could taste her over and over and still delight in the discovery of her flavor on my tongue. She sucked in a tight breath as I suckled that tiny, swollen pleasure nub, loving how her hands twisted and pulled at the bedding, her thighs shaking and trembling as I pushed her harder toward her climax.

I lost myself in her shuddering cries, drinking in her pleasure as she shattered beneath my tongue. Before she could recover, I flipped her onto her belly, taking a brief moment to admire the perfection of her ass, then went to reach for a condom, but before my fingers reached the bowl, I hesitated.

It was wrong, but a part of me knew that if I got Katherine pregnant, I'd never lose her. A baby might be the only foolproof way to get her to marry me.

But even as the ruthless Donato creed—Win at All Costs—urged me to simply drive myself unprotected into her womb, I couldn't do it.

Doing so would betray her trust in the worst way, and we'd never recover. If I was going to win her heart, I had to show her that I would never sacrifice her wants and needs for my own.

Not even if it meant losing so *she* could win.

I grabbed a condom and slid it over my erect cock

before feeding my shaft to her hot, wet southern mouth. Her folds swallowed my cock, and I lost myself in the exquisite torture of being inside the woman who was my entire world.

If I were lucky, someday Katherine would give me fine sons, strong, smart and capable. She would grace me with incredible daughters who would keep me on my toes and make me wish for the opportunity to be the man that my little girls would believe I was.

I would not be like my father. I would be kind and loving and adoring to my children.

But that wasn't tonight.

Her hot sheath closed around my cock, a tight, wondrous fit. We were made for each other. I lost myself in the pleasure of knowing that she, in this moment, was completely mine. In this bubble of sheer perfection, hiding within Malvagio's walls, I lost myself in everything that was incredible about this woman. The smell of her musk on the air was sweeter than French vanilla.

I would fuck her raw and give her such incredible bone-melting pleasure that all she could think of was when she would get her next fix. By the end of this week, I would have her so cock-drunk that she would not know where I stopped and she began.

I came quickly with violent spasms, spending completely inside her. Relief that I hadn't made a terrible choice in a weak moment made me cling to her all the more. I'd come so close to fucking everything up before I'd had a chance to show her that I was worthy of being her husband.

Thank you, God, for knocking some sense into me, I thought with a grateful heart.

But I wouldn't lie—the thought of Katherine carrying my child was the most incredibly mind-blowing concept. How ironic that I'd spent my adult sexual history doing everything that I could to prevent an accidental pregnancy, but now I wanted nothing more than Katherine swelling with my child.

I was jumping the gun. I hadn't won her heart yet. I couldn't start registering in the baby department at Neiman Marcus.

At our core we were still animals. Turned on by scent, aroused by the visual cues of a soft pussy and beautiful tits. Katherine was physically perfect in every way. And I didn't mean that in some generic, plastic Barbie sort of way.

I loved that her hips had grown faster than her body could handle. Those tiny silvery lines that she deemed imperfections were absolutely beautiful to me.

And when she swelled with my child, I would lovingly bathe her with any oil or cream or anything she desired just so I could worship her body.

Instead of going through the motions of my mother's silly courtship rituals, I should've been doing exactly what I was doing right now. Loving the shit out of her. Fucking her so hard and so often that all she could think of was me.

Instead, because of my arrogance, I'd half-heartedly followed a stupid plan set up by my parents with the belief that Katherine would come around eventually.

I'd known this woman nearly her entire life, but

maybe I'd never truly known her at all. If anyone was having an epiphany, it was me. I was thunderstruck. And all of this happened in the flash of a blinding orgasm, when everything came together in a giant cataclysm of emotion, physical response and striking clarity.

I couldn't even gasp her name, but I was screaming it in my head. Never in my life had I lost myself like this. It was scary and heady at the same time, but there was something so visceral about the way we came together.

Katherine would have to come to grips with the fact that I would chase her to the ends of the earth and take every opportunity to seduce her into loving me again if need be.

Katherine was hardwired for me, even if she didn't know it yet.

I collapsed and rolled to my back, gasping hard. Neither of us spoke. The faint sound of music from the upper floor was the only sound. The air was dense with the energy we had created together. I knew she could feel it, too. I slowly turned to regard her, waiting.

Something had changed between us. Something deep.

Did she feel it, too? Of course she did. Was that fear I saw in her eyes? No. It was something else, maybe something she wasn't ready to put a name to or define. I caressed her jaw in silent understanding. There was so much I wanted to say, so much I wanted her to know. But it was too soon. Too soon for her to recognize that she and I were meant to be together. And so I simply waited.

When she said to me in a small voice tinged with

happy exhaustion, "I'm starving," all I could do was hold her in my arms with a grateful chuckle, feeling as if I'd just been given the secret to eternal happiness—a redhead with a voracious appetite.

My woman wanted food. Damn straight that was what she was going to get.

CHAPTER SEVENTEEN

Katherine

I WAS FALLING AGAIN. Maybe I'd overestimated the depth of my disdain for anything associated with the Donato family. My own arrogance had led my heart to betray me.

I'd been so adamant that I would never be that stupid girl who begged and scraped for Luca's affection when he grew tired of me. I wasn't so naive as to believe that his interest would never wane.

Rich men were accustomed to having whatever they wanted at the snap of a finger, so when someone didn't fall at their feet, it was the challenge of the chase that interested them, not the actual person.

I'd seen it a million times. The chase was fun, the catch boring.

But Luca's game face was pretty convincing. Even if the small voice in my head kept whispering that it was all a lie, my body insisted what was happening was real.

That shattered part of myself was finally coming back together, puzzle pieces sliding together as if drawn by magnets. I would never forget how this moment felt—no matter if I died an old woman surrounded by cats or if a crosstown bus mowed me down tomorrow.

This was classic addiction behavior, and Luca was either the drug or the dealer—maybe both.

I was better than this. Stronger.

Maybe if I kept telling myself that, I would believe it.

I was losing my mind.

"What if I said I never want to leave this room?" I murmured, no longer in control of what flew from my mouth. I glanced at him quickly to gauge his reaction. I wasn't disappointed.

"I would say that I felt the same way."

The intense truth in his blue-eyed gaze struck me to the core, and I melted fresh.

Damn the Donato charm—it was their gift when they chose to use it. Dangerous if you didn't arm yourself against it.

Even sweet Nico, one of my oldest friends, had broken so many hearts it should be a crime.

But safe in this bubble with Luca, I could savor this moment for the simple pleasure that it was.

I could just wrap my legs around him and be in this moment and nowhere else.

"A quiet woman is a thinking woman," Luca said, regarding me with a subtle smile. "Should I be worried?"

I chuckled, but he was right. My thoughts were racing. I closed my arms around him, snuggling close. I was still going to walk away, but I wanted to savor the way it felt when he touched me, the way my skin ignited, the way my nerve endings came alive—the way my heart stopped in exquisite agony.

We fit together so perfectly, so poetically. I wanted to find someone else who touched me the way Luca did, but I knew I wouldn't.

My previous relationships had all lacked substance and I'd been eager and ready to let them go when the time came, because Luca had always managed to occupy space in my heart, no matter how many times I'd tried to oust him.

"Has the world landed on your shoulders?" Luca asked as he rose to grab a handful of green grapes from a decorative bowl on the marble-topped entry table. He popped a grape into his mouth, offering me one. I chewed slowly, holding his gaze.

Luca knew me so well—my subtle nuances, the things that I wanted to hide.

"I know enough to admit that what we have isn't normal, that our situation was never normal and never would be. What if what I want is something more mundane than what you could give me?"

"Clarify."

Was I ready to jump into the deep end of the pool? I supposed I owed Luca some sort of explanation, some kind of closure. I drew a deep breath and let it out slowly, gaining strength before beginning. "Luca, I don't see myself raising my kids in an environment where extreme wealth is the norm. I want my kids to have a normal life, the life I wasn't given. Now, before you get all pissy because you think I'm judging you for something you couldn't control, just listen to me. I want a normal life for my children, and I don't think you'd recognize normal if it had a sticker on its forehead."

"I'd say normal is subjective," he countered, his gaze narrowing just enough to give away his irritation.

"Did you know that I put myself on a reasonable budget when I was in college? Even though I had access to a trust fund and I could've lived large just like everyone else in our fucked-up little circles, I didn't want to. I wanted to live like a normal student. I learned a lot about life that I was oblivious to before that decision. I had the opportunity to meet people who struggled and yet still managed to make a difference in other people's lives. It made me realize that some challenges were a blessing, and I know you will never understand that concept."

"Good grief, Katherine, don't try to sell a romanticized version of strife to me. Everyone has obstacles, no matter the size of their pocketbook. Your point is both shallow and naive."

I blinked back the sudden hot tears that threatened. Why did his opinion still have the power to cut me off at the knees? Lifting my chin, I continued, undeterred, "Your elitist attitude only proves my point further. Struggle has never been part of your vocabulary, and I'm not saying it's your fault. I'm just saying that I don't want to raise my kids in that environment. And let's be real, Luca, there's no way that you would be willing to live in a modest home instead of a palatial compound that displays your wealth to the entire world just so that your children could live in a way that is relatable to ninety-nine percent of the world."

A wry, almost patronizing smirk toyed with the corners of his mouth as he reminded me, "I backpacked across Europe with nothing more than what I could carry. I've seen plenty of struggle, and I also know there's little to romanticize about it."

"At any given moment, you could've had money wired to you," I refuted, shaking my head. "Not the same. That was just more Donato playtime. You always knew that you could pick up the phone and have a private jet drop out of the sky to pick you up and change whatever situation was happening at the moment. There was no danger, no threat to your well-being. You will never know what it means to have to reach down inside you and pull out grit and raw determination to survive."

"Neither do you."

I stared, momentarily quiet before conceding his point. "Perhaps you're right. I walked away from wealth, but I knew it was always available. I knew that I could access a bank account and get what I needed. I chose not to touch the trust so I could learn how to stick to a budget, and there were times I had nothing but ramen noodles to eat for days because they were the cheapest food I could find and still pay my rent. That's what I'm talking about."

I seemed to have hit a nerve.

"Katherine," he said, his clipped tone accentuating each consonant, "I am trying to drag a company that is mired in the past into the twenty-first century so we can evolve. I'm fighting my own father to let loose of the reins so I can make things happen, but the *son of a bitch* is tenacious as fuck. I don't want my kids used as bartering chips like you and I were. For fuck's sake, I want my kids to know what it's like to simply fall in love with whomever they choose, but I can't do that. Not until I have some control—which my father refuses to relinquish—and the freedom to refashion our business into something we can all be proud of. Dante is breathing down my neck, and my father gets some sick pleasure from threatening to make Dante his heir. So I have to bide my time walking the line between forward progress and whatever my father wants, and chasing after you hasn't helped matters. So, yeah, I know *struggle*, even if I've never had to pick between eating a meal and paying rent."

His impassioned response was more than I'd expected. He so rarely talked about his stresses, I guess I'd convinced myself he didn't have any. I couldn't wrap my head around the possibility that Luca felt the same way as I did—that he wanted something more for his kids.

God, at one point I'd dreamed of our babies. I'd dreamed of what it would be like to look into the eyes of my child and see Luca staring back at me. I held back the tears that threatened to betray the depth of my yearning.

"Luca, I *hate* all of the circles you run with. Most of those people are assholes and entitled bitches. I can't deal with that lifestyle. I want a small house that I can clean myself. I want to do laundry and make dinner. I want to have a career and take care of my own children. When I go on vacation with my family, I want to pile into a minivan and go on a road trip, not some crazy ostentatious private island bullshit. My kids will not attend private school, and they will understand that whatever they want in life they have to work for. Does that sound anything like something you could provide?"

Luca blew out a heavy breath with a defeated shake of his head. "Katherine, what do you want me to say? We were born into wealthy, well-connected families, and nothing can change that. I want to give my kids the best I can provide them with. I don't want them to want for anything. Fine, we'll buy a fucking house in the ghetto someplace so we can raise our kids next to drug dealers and prostitutes."

"That's the point. I don't want them to have everything given to them. Struggle isn't always bad."

Luca shook his head. "I don't see how struggling is good for anyone, least of all kids."

This was going nowhere. "Forget it, Luca. You and I are just too different...and we want different things."

I wanted to get dressed and leave, but Luca wasn't finished.

"Hold up," he said firmly when I moved to shimmy into my panties. "You're not going to withdraw because you're afraid of taking a chance on seeing something different that goes against what you *think* you know. You have to give people a chance in order to determine whether or not they're capable of reaching your expectations."

I ignored his pointed look and grabbed the discarded bustier, crumpled on the floor. "Life lessons aren't exactly in your wheelhouse, Luca. You should stick to what you know. Go acquire some failing corporation and tear it to pieces for scrap. Leave the heavy lifting to those who are qualified."

My barb glanced off without the desired effect. Luca's lip curled with disappointment. "I never realized how cowardly you truly are until this moment."

"Excuse me?"

"You are more willing to run from the possibility of happiness because it challenges some twisted belief you've got locked in your head than take a chance and face the unknown. That's chickenshit."

"Don't tell me what I am," I fired back. "You don't have that right. *You* broke my heart. You are the one who ruined everything. Don't sit there and condescend to me that I'm not the one willing to give people chances, because that's not true. I gave you everything that was mine to give and I loved you, Luca, and you cheated on me!"

Crap! I bounded away from him, jerking on the ridiculous lingerie I'd worn into Malvagio. I felt more vulnerable and exposed than being completely nude. I didn't want Luca knowing that my feelings for him went deeper than I was willing to admit.

"I want to go home," I said, tears crowding my eyes. A mental breakdown felt imminent, or at the very least an ugly sobfest. Emotions, both good and bad, crashed into me like snowballs from every direction. "Luca, now!"

At the near-hysterical note in my voice, Luca sprang from the bed and pulled me into his arms. I wanted to push him away, but my arms had no strength. All I could do was allow him to fold me into his embrace and hold me so tight that all the broken pieces inside me had to knit back together, even as I struggled to keep them apart.

No, I wasn't ready to love him again. I wasn't ready to give him exactly what he wanted. He could not win!

Finding my strength, I pushed against him. "Stop. I want to go home."

Luca let me go. "Home? And where is home? You have no home here in California. You left without any solid plans. You're so goddamn hotheaded you didn't think this through."

Luca stalked away from me, striding naked to the bathroom. The slamming door echoed behind him. Alone in the room, I let the tears fall. He was right.

I was scared. I was hotheaded. I was reactionary.

And in that moment I felt like I'd gotten everything wrong—which I hated even more.

How could he possibly turn the argument around so that I was the one who felt terrible? As if I'd based my opinions on fake news and gossip.

There was nothing fake about the ache in my heart. The memory of seeing that woman perched on my boyfriend's lap, immortalized in print for everyone to gawk at, was still very clear in my mind.

I could almost look back and say, *You know what, we were both young and stupid.* But that did nothing to ease the pain and the suffering I went through after he broke me!

I was damaged because of him, and it was hard for me to wrap my brain around the fact that the person who had damaged me the most was the one I still wanted.

Luca reappeared, a specimen of male perfection even as every muscle was rigid and taut with anger. No matter what, he still had the power to take my breath away. I supposed I could add that to the stack of crosses I had to bear when it came to Luca.

Seemed fitting, because the truth was pretty brutal.

No matter how far I ran, I would never escape the fact that Luca would always be in my heart.

CHAPTER EIGHTEEN

Luca

THE RETURN RIDE to the hotel was silent. I'd lost all the
ground I'd gained, and I was kicking myself for playing my hand too soon.

I could practically feel Katherine vibrating with
anger and hurt, too many memories from the past standing between us.

If I tried to explain, it would come off as justifica-
tions, and that was the last thing she wanted to hear
right now.

I wasn't going to grovel over an incident that was so
fucking stupid it was practically a nonissue. I hadn't
cheated on Katherine—I'd never even kissed that
woman—but appearances were everything, and she'd
been on my lap, topless.

What Katherine didn't know was that immediately
after the paparazzi took the picture, I removed the
drunken starlet from my lap and went to unload the te-
quila I'd downed as I'd puked my guts out.

I'd tried to tell Katherine, but when she hadn't believed me, I hadn't tried very hard to fix the misunderstanding. Like I said, I'd been shamefully relieved.

Maybe I'd wanted to be free for a time before getting married.

Maybe subconsciously I'd wanted Katherine to experience more of life before tying herself to me for the rest of her life.

Hell, I could spend hours coming up with a dozen different scenarios that might justify why I hadn't just tried a little bit harder to clear the air and heal the hurt.

But at the end of the day, my silence had been the loudest.

I half expected her to take a stand and demand that I take the pullout sofa in the living room of the suite rather than the sumptuous luxury king, but she didn't, even if her glance did flick to the sofa before she trudged to the bedroom.

I supposed that was a good sign, right? *Better not count your blessings just yet.*

"Are we going to talk about this?" I ventured, removing my shirt and tossing it, peeling myself from the leather pants with equal disregard for where they ended up.

"Nope," she answered, disappearing behind the bathroom door with her nightclothes. I much preferred her naked, but the chances of that happening were slim to none.

I sighed and removed my watch, setting it on the nightstand, and climbed into the bed. Katherine reappeared a few moments later, her face scrubbed, her hair tied up in a bun. If she thought she was going to deter me by going with the schoolmarm look, she was sadly mistaken.

What my future bride didn't realize was that she could be wearing a paper sack and I'd still find her the sexiest creature alive. Even if she wasn't the friendliest at the moment.

"Kath—"

"I'm tired."

I shut my mouth. Nothing was going to happen tonight. Tomorrow would be about damage control.

I had a plan. All I had to do was follow through and see it done. My eyes drifted shut, and I found sleep relatively quickly.

So quickly, in fact, that morning came within a blink.

I awoke to an empty bed, alarm chasing the sleep from my brain. Bounding from the bed, I called out for Katherine, only to find her at the table, sipping her tea and reading the delivered newspaper, fully dressed as if she'd risen hours before me.

The little vixen hadn't wanted to leave anything to chance. She'd known if given a shot I would find a way to make love to her again, and this was her way of thwarting me.

Well, I wasn't so easily deterred. "I never took you for an early bird. What happened to the girl who said she was a night owl?"

"She grew up."

A short and sweet answer delivered with a perfunctory and bland smile.

"Good," I said, surprising her when I didn't engage as she'd hoped. "I have big plans for today."

"As do I, seeing as it's my turn to pick our activities," she said with another smile, only this time there was an edge to the corners. "Today, we are going to volunteer at a local soup kitchen."

No, today we were going to Sonoma County. "Yes, technically, it is your day," I conceded, rubbing my chin at the dilemma. "I guess I overestimated how much you would enjoy spending the day at Coppola's winery... We had so much fun last night at Cafe Zoetrope that I got ahead of myself and booked a private tour. But I can cancel. Volunteering at a soup kitchen sounds equally fun."

I knew her weaknesses.

"It's impossible to get a private tour on such short notice," she said, calling my bluff.

"For a Donato, nothing is impossible," I reminded her with a shrug. "Our tour is scheduled for this afternoon, which means we need to get moving if we want to make it to Geyersville on time."

"I know what you're doing," she said, narrowing her eyes. "And it's not going to work."

I was a bastard and probably going to hell, but it would be worth it. I tried to make the decision easier for her. "How about a compromise?"

"What do you mean?"

"Helping others is the main goal when you volunteer, but there are other ways to help... Would it ease your conscience if I wrote a fat check to the shelter of your choice so that we could go enjoy our day without the guilt?"

"You can't just toss out money everywhere you go

to solve your problems," she said with a scowl, my plan backfiring. "Coppola will just have to wait. We are going to the soup kitchen."

The firm set of her jaw told me she would rather cut off her nose to spite her face than admit she'd much rather spend the day in Geyersville. I silently swore at her damn stubborn nature, but a deal was a deal.

I sighed. "I'll make some calls. Coppola will be disappointed. There aren't many filmmakers who are willing to personally give the tour, but I'm sure he'll understand."

Katherine's jaw dropped a little, but she didn't take it back, even though it was killing her. "Francis Ford Coppola was going to give the tour?" she asked, wincing. "Are you kidding me?"

"No, but it was a onetime deal. He's a busy guy, as you can imagine. Anyway, I'm going to shower and then we can be off."

I smothered the chuckle bubbling to the surface and left her to think about what she'd just sacrificed for her stubborn pride.

Soup kitchen, here we come.

CHAPTER NINETEEN

Katherine

WITHOUT REALIZING IT, Luca had made my point. He was much more willing to throw money at something than experience it himself if the situation didn't align with his personal comfort. There was no growth or learning curve in cheating the experience like that. I didn't want my children to learn that lesson, either.

But to be honest, I'd thrown out the soup kitchen idea believing that Luca would refuse. Charity I was familiar with—I'd been to more charity balls and benefits than I could count. Giving time had always seemed more genuine to me than giving money, but I'd never actually done it before. Why? I'd never been in a homeless shelter, just as I'd never actually slept in a hostel before the other night, either.

And so far I was not all that enthused with what I'd discovered, which only made me feel like a spoiled diva—the one thing I was trying my damnedest not to be.

When Luca reappeared, dressed and ready to roll, I

averted my gaze when I felt the urge to stare with longing. The man could make anything look like the height
of fashion, even jeans and a soft gray henley.

My mouth dried as memories of that hot body jabbed
at me. How could I be so addicted to his touch, even
after all these years? It was as if no one had ever existed
until Luca touched me. Total bullshit. Especially after
last night had gone down in flames. I was above that
moony girl stuff, and I would prove it by completely
squashing those irritating tingles dancing in the pit of
my stomach.

"You ready?" I asked, grabbing my purse.

"As ready as I'll ever be," he answered with a grin
that melted me just a little.

Grateful that Luca didn't feel compelled to talk about
last night, I spun on my heel before he could start. "Let's
hit the road, then. Our ride is waiting." It seemed highly
inappropriate to arrive at a homeless shelter in a town
car, so I'd ordered an Uber. Secretly, I was hoping
that Luca was appalled, but he wasn't. The damn man
climbed into the modest sedan without blinking an eye.
"You can still change your mind," I told him. "It won't
hurt my feelings at all."

"I'm looking forward to experiencing an adventure with you," he replied, and I nearly swallowed my
tongue.

"It will probably smell," I said, trying to paint a picture that wouldn't appeal to him. "And the people will
probably smell, too."

"Probably."

"And that doesn't bother you?"

He shrugged. "Human beings without access to showers and basic hygiene products generally smell. I'd smell just as bad, if not worse, if I couldn't shower and brush my teeth." He cast a smile my way, adding, "Even you would stink. Humans are dirty creatures."

Who was this guy? I nodded but didn't trust my voice, grateful when I didn't have to find something to fill the silence, because we'd arrived.

The building, covered in graffiti, was nothing to look at from the outside, but I'd read that this particular shelter was known for accepting anyone, even drug addicts and criminals, if they were in need and there was a bed available.

Run by the sisters of the Immaculate Conception Nunnery, the shelter was bustling by the time we walked in. I'd already set up the volunteer hours with Sister Mary over the phone, so after being directed to her office, we found ourselves seated opposite a stout older woman with a rather stern countenance.

I could totally imagine Sister Mary wielding a ruler to slap the knuckles of unruly children.

"Welcome to our humble shelter," Sister Mary said, her round face breaking into a brief smile. "We appreciate new volunteers."

"Happy to help," I murmured, shooting a glance at Luca. Was he going to throw his checkbook at her, or would he go through with volunteering? I held my breath, waiting.

"My fiancée is so kindhearted she insisted we spend some of our vacation helping those less fortunate," Luca said. "I'll admit it wasn't my first choice, but now that

I'm here, I'm looking forward to getting my hands dirty."

Sister Mary smiled with approval. "That's a good man," she said for my benefit, and I wanted to roll my eyes but didn't. She produced some paperwork and slid it over to us. "I just need you to sign a few forms, acknowledging that you are choosing to volunteer and that you will not hold the Immaculate Conception Nunnery responsible for any injuries you may sustain while in service."

"Injuries?" I repeated with a confused frown. "What do you mean?"

Sister Mary folded her hands and answered, "My dear, sometimes our guests are unstable. They can't help themselves—they are unwell. We do our best to keep our volunteers safe, but sometimes a guest will become unruly and scuffles happen. But not to worry, we have security for those events and rarely does anything truly harmful occur. However—" she tapped the documents "—we all have to take precautions so we can continue our good work."

I nodded and signed my name, but maybe I'd bitten off more than I could chew. I looked to Luca, but he didn't seem deterred in the least. In fact, he looked ready to get started. His strong, solid signature sealed the deal for the both of us, and I realized this was happening.

I wrestled with the cowardly urge to back out. Nothing was working as I'd planned. Luca wasn't playing his part as expected. Each time I thought I had him pegged, he spun around and did something completely out of character, challenging what I thought I knew, and that was beyond dangerous.

I was already teetering on the edge of the cliff—a part of me had never stopped loving Luca—but I didn't want to be roped into the Donato family lifestyle and obligations. I shuddered, hating the thought of Luca becoming anything like his father. If it weren't for those undeniably strong Donato genes, I'd question whether or not Giovanni's blood ran through Luca's veins.

Wouldn't that be a kick in the pants for the old man if it turned out Luca was someone else's kid? I smothered an inappropriate giggle. My nerves were jangled enough to show through the mask I was hiding behind, and Luca could see I was struggling, plain as day.

I didn't know which was worse, realizing that I wasn't as bohemian as I tried to be or that Luca could see right through me.

I guess it didn't matter. I was going to see this through, simply because I refused to let Luca have the last laugh.

Accepting gloves and an apron with forced cheer, I followed Sister Mary into the dining hall, where the rest of the volunteers were already serving breakfast.

But when I expected the nun to put us together, she sent Luca in one direction and me in another.

I chewed my lip, watching as Luca went off with a smiling volunteer with big, bouncy red hair and even bouncier boobs, and I was delivered to a not-so-smiley nun with a pinched mouth and hard eyes.

Within a heartbeat, I'd been sized up and found wanting, but another set of hands was still useful.

"This is Sister Bernice," Sister Mary said in quick introduction. "She'll be your supervisor today. Sister Bernice, this is Katherine. Have a blessed day and thank you for your contribution."

And then Sister Mary left me with the battle-ax.

"We're kitchen detail," Sister Bernice said flatly, turning and expecting me to follow, which I reluctantly did. We rounded the corner and entered a huge working kitchen, bustling with activity. Everywhere I looked, people were passing to and fro, hands filled with giant bowls of food, heading for the serving hall. I figured I was going to be cooking or chopping, something food related, but when Sister Bernice pointed to the stack of dishes crowding the oversize sink, I felt like Cinderella staring at an impossible workload, except I didn't have any mice or birds to help me with the job.

"I'm pretty good with cutting and chopping," I offered helpfully. "I can chop with the best of them."

"We have all the choppers we need," Bernice stated with a brief lift of her lips that might have passed for a smile in a different life. "We need someone to wash dishes."

"Of course. No problem." I offered a wan smile and went to the monster sink and the mile-high dishes crusted with food. I slipped the rubber gloves on and grabbed the industrial-size nozzle to start rinsing.

Each time I cleared a spot, another cartful of dishes appeared, until I couldn't pretend to smile anymore, but I didn't quit. Quitting would only prove that I was exactly the type of person I didn't want to be. Maybe all this time I'd been playing the part of an independent woman, knowing full well that I could access my trust at any time. Just like Luca had accused.

I used my forearm to wipe the sweat from my forehead before it dripped into my eye. It was cold as a witch's tit outside, but in this kitchen, it was roasting.

"You look thirsty," a voice said. I turned and saw a young man offering a bottled water, which I gratefully accepted. "How'd you end up on dish duty? You give Sister Bernice attitude or something?"

I chuckled, shaking my head. "I didn't say two words to her before she sized me up and stuck me here." I guzzled the water, out of breath by the last swallow. "Thanks," I said, smiling. "My name's Katherine. What's yours?"

"Bart," he answered, extending his hand in welcome. "Let me guess…community service for…a drunken sorority prank?"

I laughed. "No, I came because I thought it would—" *make my fiancé run back to New York* "—be fun."

"Are you having fun?" he asked, his brow rising. "Because you look miserable."

I started to protest, but I didn't have the energy to lie. "I'm…totally miserable," I admitted. "So why are you here?"

"Community service. Drunken frat prank," he answered with a wink. "Anyway, the sisters are always good for signing off on community service, so they have a pretty steady stream of volunteers to put to work."

"Spoken by a repeat offender?"

Bart shrugged without commitment, but the imp-

ALEXX ANDRIA   175

ish grin said it all. "So, you're not from here... Let me guess... East Coast? Maybe New York?"

"Does my accent give me away?"

"A little." He made a pinching gesture with his fingers. "But it's cute. I love girls with accents."

I laughed, shaking my head. Bart was definitely flirting, but when I realized that my first thought was I wished Luca could see a cute guy flirting with me, I knew I was officially a terrible person. "I'm here with my fiancé," I said, letting Bart down gently. "He got lucky. Sister Mary sent him to the serving hall."

"Fiancé?" He groaned, covering his heart as if shot. "Just my luck. All right, whoever he is, he's one lucky bastard."

Divulging the odd truth of my relationship with Luca would only serve to create more questions I couldn't answer, so I just smiled and nodded in thanks.

"Let me see your hands," Bart said. When I simply stared quizzically, he laughed and repeated his request, adding, "I promise it's nothing weird." More curious than anything else, I removed my rubber gloves. Bart grasped my hands and turned them this way and that, finally revealing his reason. "Sister Bernice always puts the people with the softest hands in the kitchen, and the ones she thinks need the most humbling, she puts on dishes."

My mouth gaped. "Me? Why would *I* need humbling? It was my idea to volunteer."

"Let me tell you, Sister Bernice has the eyes of a hawk. She can see what others can't."

The heat crept into my cheeks. I'd been judged?

How was it possible that *I'd* failed the test while Luca had passed with flying colors? I rolled my shoulders to release the gathering tension. "Well, I can guarantee Luca's hands are softer than mine," I groused, but I knew that probably wasn't true. Luca loved being active, and he wasn't afraid to get his hands dirty.

"New college grad?" Bart surmised with a knowing grin. Not as new as he thought, but a close guess. "You have that highly educated but ultimately useless look about you." My pride pinched, I scowled in response, but Bart just laughed. "Hey, not judging, cutie, just making an observation. My older brother has that same look, and I have no doubt as soon as I graduate in the spring I'll have that look, too. I think it comes with the degree. After this last shenanigan, my dad put his foot down, saying, *It's time to get serious, son,*" he said, in a mockingly parental tone. "But, I don't know, nothing really grabs me."

"Actually, I had a job with a high-powered marketing firm, Franklin and Dodd, but I quit to come to California. I'm thinking of a career change."

"Brave," Bart said. "Your fiancé cool with that?"

"It's not his decision, it's mine, but...yeah, I think he's okay with it." Luca didn't care where I worked. He just wanted me to marry him. The quiet truth hit me hard. This trip hadn't exactly turned out as I'd expected. It was a sobering thing to realize that the soapbox you were perched on was quickly breaking down. I'd spent a long time believing that I was unequivocally right about certain things, but Luca had me questioning what I thought I knew.

Bart and I were fairly close in age, but unlike him, I didn't suffer from a lack of ambition or drive. If anything, I had more than I could possibly put to good use, which was why the thought of becoming a society matron scraped at my last nerve. I didn't want to be a useless piece of arm candy.

"That your man coming toward us with a look like he wants to beat me with my own arm?" Bart asked with fake fright. "Jesus, he's tall."

I hid the smile that immediately bloomed. Yes, Luca was delightfully tall and broad shouldered. And he did, indeed, look as if he might want to thrash Bart for flirting with me. A warm tickle danced in my belly. There was something undeniably sexy about the way Luca looked at me. Sometimes when his blue eyes fixed on mine, I felt as if he could see straight to my soul.

I smothered the wistful sigh that threatened.

None of that.

"I came to ask if you'd like to sign on for another four-hour shift or if you'd like to go," Luca said, shooting a cool look Bart's way.

Bart thrust his hand toward Luca. "Bart's the name, and you, big guy, are one lucky son of a bitch for locking down this hottie."

My cheeks heated, but I laughed. To my surprise, Luca's tension released and he accepted the hand offered. "Pleasure, Bart. And yes—" his gaze flitted to me with warmth "—I'm a lucky man."

Bart grinned and said, "Well, I've still got another four hours on my tab, so I'd better find Sister Mean Eyes and get my assignment. I'd say you two did your good deed for the day—go find something more interesting to do. I know what I'd be doing if she was my girl…" He sauntered off with a wink.

My amused smile caused Luca to pull me into his arms, circling my waist possessively before I could stop him. "I can't leave you alone for a second," he murmured with a low growl, sending shivers down my back. His lips nibbled at the soft skin of my neck, and my knees threatened to buckle. "Stay or go?" he asked.

"Go," I answered breathlessly.

Luca pulled away, his lips twitching with knowing, but I didn't care. I didn't want to wash dishes anymore, and at the moment I didn't care to examine my reasoning with a magnifying glass.

"Good." Luca grabbed my hand and led me from the hot, stifling kitchen to sign us out with Sister Mary. "You do good work here," he told the nun as he handed her a business card. "Call my office on Monday for a proper donation."

"Bless you, Mr. Donato," Sister Mary said. "Thank you for your service and donation."

Luca dipped his head in acknowledgment and we left the shelter, only this time Luca had called for the town car.

As I settled into the plush back seat, a question nagged at me.

Was I fighting out of spite, or was this a battle truly worth fighting?

At this point…I didn't know anymore.

CHAPTER TWENTY

Luca

I'D ONLY EVER been territorial with one woman, and that was Katherine. I knew there was nothing to the harmless flirting between Katherine and the smiley-eyed little bastard, but that didn't stop my teeth from baring. It wasn't that she was talking to another man…it was the fact that a stranger could so easily make her smile and laugh when all I could do was make her suspicious of my motives.

Spare me the lecture. Yeah, I knew this was a problem of my own making, but that didn't make it any less difficult to deal with, and right now, all I wanted was to feel Katherine beneath me.

I drew her to me, my hand cupping the back of her neck, and sealed my mouth to hers, letting my hunger override any hint of cunning or strategy. My tongue sought hers, tangling and twisting with an urgency that she could feel in my touch. When she responded in kind, my cock hardened to stone, violently ready to pin her to the motherfucking black leather.

"L-Luca," she breathed against my mouth, pushing against my chest with furtive glances at the driver, who was doing his best to keep his eyes on the road. "What are you doing?"

"Isn't it obvious?" I asked, toying with the buttons on her jeans.

She gasped. "But the driver," she whispered, covering my hands with hers.

"The driver is paid to mind his own fucking business," I growled, dipping forward to kiss the base of her throat. Leaning back to catch her eye, I asked, "May I?"

She gave a furtive glance to the front seat before turning to me again. "Yes. God, yes," she said, scrambling to unbutton her jeans.

I reached for her jeans and panties, swiftly tugging them down and off completely, responding to the way her body quickened to my touch. I could smell her arousal, that sweet, musky feminine grace that only Katherine possessed. I grabbed her legs and pulled her to her back, one leg splayed over the seat, the other anchored over my shoulder as I nibbled my way to her tight pussy.

"Oh, God," Katherine moaned, clapping her hand over her eyes as her teeth worried her bottom lip. I dipped a finger inside her, withdrew and licked her essence clean, groaning with pleasure. Katherine was sweetness personified. I couldn't wait any longer. My hunger wouldn't wait. I needed to feel her shatter so I could drown in her release. I went straight for the tiny, swollen piece of her that throbbed beneath my tongue, sucking and teasing until her entire body was shaking and twitching with each stroke. Her skin dampened as her breath became stilted, muscles tensing. I wanted to draw it out, tease her until she was mindless, but I couldn't help myself. I was delirious with the taste and sound of her and I couldn't stop.

Come for me, baby.

As if hearing my silent demand, Katherine stiffened and cried out as she hit her climax, gripping the seat cushion for dear life as her entire body spasmed. She gasped, her mouth falling open as her chest rose and fell like a boat on a turbulent sea, but I wasn't satisfied. I needed to be inside her, to take her as only I could. No one touched her like I did, and I knew that for a fact.

I moved away from her so I could release my cock, popping the buttons on my jeans with shaking fingers. No sooner had I sprung free and sheathed myself with a condom than Katherine climbed on top, knees straddling me so I could slide in.

Her honeyed pussy sucked me into her body, and I groaned as intense pleasure gripped my cock. I clutched her hips as she moved, rubbing herself against my shaft, her cheeks flushed and her hair wild. The air in the car became stuffy, but the driver knew well enough to keep his fingers away from that window divider switch that maintained the barrier between us. I wanted to taste, smell and immerse myself in everything that was Katherine.

I wanted to lick the sweat from her body, swallow the cries from her mouth. She rocked against me, finding her own pleasure even as I rocketed toward mine. I was inside her—heaven—just me and her. This was how we connected and how we'd always connect. Our bodies knew the truth even if neither of us was willing to commit to the words.

Katherine braced herself on the ceiling as I anchored her hips; her thrusts became erratic and I surged inside her. The liquid heat between us pooled and sizzled until I couldn't hold back any longer. I jetted hard, straining with the effort it took to keep from breaking the windows. Dimly, I heard Katherine follow with a feminine cry, slumping against me, her head lolling on my shoulder as her walls pulsed around me, milking every drop from my balls.

My arms closed around her, my cock still buried deep. I could sleep for days just like this.

Primal emotion flooded me. I would fuck her raw if given the chance, not only because fucking her felt right, but because I simply couldn't get enough.

"Air, please," I said, my voice raw, and the driver discreetly levered the window to allow some fresh air to circulate. It was then Katherine came to her senses and met my gaze, her embarrassment evident, but I simply kissed her again, saying, "Wealth has its privileges."

That, she couldn't deny, and she didn't try.

Nodding, she slowly climbed from my lap.

As we adjusted our clothing, Katherine said, "You're making mincemeat out of my declaration that I wouldn't have sex with you."

We broke into shared laughter as I said, "I never take my eye off the prize." I buttoned the final button on my jeans, saying, "And if you really want to know, I'll admit that I plan to fuck you at any opportunity given me." Color flushed her cheeks prettily. I took a chance and added, "But tell me if I'm wrong... I don't think you mind."

"I don't," she admitted with an unhappy sigh, tucking her feet up under her. "That's the thing, Luca...sexual chemistry was never our problem. Our problems were much bigger and went way deeper."

"You said *deeper*," I teased, cracking a reluctant smile from her lips.

"I'm being serious."

I exhaled. "Yeah, well, most couples do have problems. We're not immune."

"We're not a couple, Luca."

I met her gaze. "What do you want, Katherine? An apology? Do you want to hear that I would change things if I could? That I would take back hurting you? Yeah, I would do anything to take back what happened on that damn yacht, but I'll never apologize for wanting to marry you. I want you, Katherine. It's always been you. I don't really give a shit how it came about... maybe we were always destined to find each other and this was just the particular way things shook out for us, but I don't care. I love you."

The words tumbled from my mouth without forethought. I confess, I'd thrown around the *L* word before, but there'd been nothing behind it. Only when I thought of Katherine did the word take on a different meaning, hold a significant weight.

And I'd never said those words to *her*. Not even when we were younger. I'd always said things like "There's no one like you" or "You're my number one girl," which

Katherine had been fine with, because she'd known that we were going to marry.

She'd said the words to me plenty of times—and I'd squirmed each time.

Not because I hadn't felt things...but because I'd felt things I wasn't ready to deal with.

I'd been a kid. Barely out of college. She'd been a teenager. Each time she'd looked at me with those stars in her eyes, I'd cringed. I hadn't been ready to jump feetfirst into what I knew was in store for the both of us. I'd told myself hurting her had been a fucked-up blessing, but in all honesty, I'd been a damn coward.

But the words were out there now, sitting between us like a fat cat that'd eaten too much cream and wasn't going anywhere.

"You shouldn't use words you don't understand," Katherine warned in a cold tone, but the bright sheen in her eyes gave her away.

Maybe it was time to actually come clean and admit what I'd always known but had been too afraid to show. It was probably lousy timing, but time wasn't something I had in surplus. I still had to deal with my father when all this was said and done. I drew a deep breath and reached for her hand. She looked at me sharply but didn't pull away, which gave me hope. "I've always loved you, Katherine. I just wasn't ready."

"What?"

"I've always loved you."

"You don't cheat on the people you love."

"I agree. I didn't cheat on you."

She looked at me sharply before pulling away, putting distance between us. "Come again?"

"I told you then, I'm telling you now... I didn't cheat on you. I was drunk. The woman sat on my lap and kissed me, but I didn't kiss her back. Right after, I removed her from my lap and promptly threw up."

"You're expecting me to believe that you had a topless Chrissy McMichael on your lap and it was totally innocent?"

"Oh, hell no, I didn't say it was innocent. I shouldn't have let her sit on my lap. It was an error in judgment, but then, I was also fucking drunk off my ass. But I didn't mean for you to be hurt."

"Convenient. Too bad you weren't willing to own up to anything back then."

"I tried telling you what really happened. You weren't interested in listening. Not that I blamed you. I'll be the first to admit it looked bad."

She didn't respond, just continued to gaze at me with reproach.

"It's the truth," I told her, laying all my cards on the table. "But I fucked up that day by not admitting what I really needed to say."

"Which was?"

"I thought it was better if we took a break. I didn't have the balls to admit that I was relieved that you broke it off."

Her eyes widened with incredulity, and she shook her head as if she couldn't quite wrap her head around my admission. "You wanted to break up?"

"Yes and no. But mostly yes. Not for the reasons you might think, though."

"Oh, I've got to hear this," Katherine mocked, fresh anger leaking into her tone. "This ought to be amazing."

"I needed you to experience life. Hell, *I* needed to experience more before I settled down so that when we did actually tie the knot, I would be ready. I wanted that for you, too."

"That's some backward-ass logic." She rubbed at her nose with a sharp, agitated motion. "I mean, Jesus, Luca, you didn't need to break my fucking heart just to get some space."

"I was stupid" was all I could say in my own defense. "I know that now, but I can't take it back. All I can do is learn from it and move forward. But be honest with yourself for a second…would you have understood if I'd said, 'Hey, babe, let's take a small break so we can both do some wild and crazy shit without each other'?"

She didn't bother lying. "No."

"See?"

"I don't even know what to think about this, Luca. How am I supposed to react to this information? Just laugh it off and say, 'Oh, all is forgiven!' because you've decided to come clean about your true reasons for hurting me?"

"I'm trying to be honest with you. If we're to have any shot together, I want to start with a clean slate," I answered quietly, because it was the truth. "I don't want to keep anything from you ever again. A pretty lie is what started all this. I should've just knuckled down and given you the ugly truth and let the chips fall where they may. I think we would've been able to get through that far easier than what we're doing now."

"Maybe." A beat passed between us. "But that's not what happened, is it? So we have to deal with the reality of our situation."

"And the reality is?"

"I can't marry you."

I rejected her declaration, heart and soul. "You're mine and you always will be. I will chase you to the ends of the earth until you realize we were meant for one another."

Katherine threw her hands up in an exasperated motion to wipe at the tears that had begun to track down her cheeks. "This is so classic Luca. Pulling out the big guns for the win, because winning is everything. But I'm not a prize to be won. I'm a human, flesh and blood, and you broke my heart. I don't care that you weren't ready for what you were feeling. It still sliced me to ribbons, and now it feels even worse somehow, knowing that you actually hadn't cheated on me but you didn't try to convince me otherwise. You let me think that I wasn't enough for you. I don't think I can forgive you for that."

"I could say I'm sorry a million different ways, but it wouldn't change how I handled myself. All I can say is…I am so sorry for hurting you."

"Wouldn't it just be easier to let me go?" she asked in a plaintive cry that tore at my heart. "I mean, love isn't supposed to be this hard."

"Bullshit. Love is love. Whether it's hard or easy depends on how we handle what comes our way. I love you, Katherine Cerinda Oliver. I've never wanted anyone more than I want you. I'm ready to be the man you need me to be. Just give me a damn chance to show you."

"How do I know you're not just playing me to get what you want?"

"I don't chase after what I have no interest in catching. Woman, I'd chase you until we were both in wheelchairs. A lifetime doesn't seem nearly long enough for all the things I want to experience with you. Does that sound like someone who's just playing?"

"Crap," she muttered as fresh tears dribbled down her cheeks. "Now look what you've done. I'm a giant crybaby mess."

"I think you're beautiful," I said, proving it by kissing her tearstained lips. Salty and sweet, that was my Katherine. I kissed her softly, brushing my lips across hers with a tender touch. I wanted everything with her, even if it meant weathering the ups and downs of a volatile relationship. I was in, 100 percent.

I sensed the crack in her armor as she sagged against me, opening her mouth so my tongue could slide inside. Her breasts begged for my touch, and I was happy to oblige as my hand crept beneath her sweater to caress a pert, pouty breast. I wanted her nipple in my mouth, but I could wait.

Nibbling the column of her neck, I inhaled the sweetness of her skin, losing myself to the intoxicating pleasure that was solely Katherine.

"Luca," she moaned, the sound of her anguish going straight to my heart. I slowed to a stop, even though I wanted to devour her a second time. She peered at me through wet lashes. "I just can't. I'm sorry."

"Why not?" I pressed, needing to find that stubborn bone of contention stuck in her mind. "Tell me. I'll listen."

Katherine paused, gauging my response, as if testing whether or not she could trust me. The moment felt heavy—everything was riding on which path we took. Would she trust me enough to share her true fears? Or would she withdraw and push me away again?

God, Katherine, please let me in.

CHAPTER TWENTY-ONE

Katherine

HE'D SAID THE WORDS—*I'm sorry*—I'd wanted to hear for so long yet had given up hope I ever would. Donatos didn't apologize. They were stubborn and stoic, marching to the beat of their own drum. Even if I was stunned by the apology, I had to recognize the ugly truth—my problems weren't so easily solved. An apology was simply words uttered to create an effect. Luca would say and do anything to get what he wanted, that much I knew.

"How can I trust you're not saying what you think I need to hear?"

"Trust is a leap of faith. You have to let go of whatever you're holding on to in order to make that jump."

I skewed my gaze at him. "Since when did you become such a philosopher?"

"When my fiancée kept doing everything in her power to push me away."

"Why do you keep calling me your fiancée when I've

told you repeatedly that I'm not going to marry you?"
I asked, exasperated.

He chuckled. "Because I'm an optimist."

I looked away, refusing to let his charm get to me.
There was something stubbornly romantic about the
way he refused to take no for an answer. "You're impossible," I said, shaking my head. "What am I going
to do with you?"

"Marry me."

His simple answer took my breath away, and tears
started fresh.

Luca slipped his hand into mine. His gentle touch
was tender, speaking of genuine concern, but I questioned if any of it was real. Nothing felt right in my head
right now. When I'd bailed on New York, I'd known in
my heart I was making the right decision. Now? I was
turned around and upside down, and it was all because
Luca wasn't performing to the script.

It was as if we'd just stepped into a time warp and
he was once again the Luca I'd fallen in love with—
kind, funny, considerate, *sexy*…well, *that* part had never
changed—and I was falling all over again, faster than
I could stop myself.

Instead of confidence, fear was my traveling com-
panion. Fear of myself, of what I'd been denying since
Luca had broken my heart, of losing myself in the Donato vortex, fear of being exactly the kind of person I'd
been disdaining since I'd discovered that ugly mag with
my boyfriend's picture on the cover with that sloppy-
drunk starlet.

To be honest, the whole situation at the shelter had

thrown me for a loop. The person I thought I was might not be real at all. Sister Bernice had summed me up in a glance simply by looking at my hands. It pinched to be judged so quickly, but there was a level of truth to her conclusion, and that killed me inside.

"I don't like your father, and your mother is iffy," I said abruptly, readying myself for a fight, but Luca just nodded. My sails deflated.

"Sometimes my family is hard to like," he said with a shrug.

Couldn't argue with that.

"Your father scares me."

"I will never allow anyone to hurt you," Luca promised.

"What if you can't prevent it?"

His low growl surprised me. "I will break anyone who tries."

There was something real and deeply rooted behind his gaze, something I'd never seen before. Was it possible Luca truly loved me? My heart skipped a beat at the thought. I desperately wanted Luca to love me, *really* love me, not because I was his arranged bride, but because he'd chosen me above all else.

"How can you know that what you feel is genuine, that it won't fade?" I asked.

"You're the only one questioning their feelings. I've always known how I felt about you. I always knew you were the only one for me. I just had to be ready to go all in."

My eyes burned with unshed tears as my heart ached with the need to hear exactly that, but my brain was determined to question everything that came out of his mouth and I was breaking from the strain. "I can't think anymore," I cried, losing it. "I just can't. Luca, I—"

"Shh," he crooned, drawing me into his arms. "Then don't think. Just let me do the thinking for now. We're on our way to wine country, where we are going to enjoy being tourists, okay? I want you to think of nothing more than which wine you want to sample next. No more picking at problems bigger than whatever the moment can provide."

It sounded so tempting—turn off the brain and just enjoy the day with the man I was impossibly crazy about—but could I actually do it? God, I wanted to enjoy this day with Luca. I wanted to hold his hand and walk through the vineyards, eat good food and laugh at silly jokes.

So do it.

The voice I'd been trying to ignore was louder than my fears this time.

I wiped at my tears, nodding slowly. "Okay," I said, swallowing the lump in my throat. "I can do that. I think."

Luca smiled and kissed me again.

Everything felt right when his lips were on mine. Was it possible to say *screw the world* and just chase my happiness?

Could I convince Luca that a life with me was better than a life slaved to his family? Was I really going to ask Luca to choose between me and the Donato empire?

Two seconds into my attempt to stop thinking, I was already breaking the rules. I exhaled a long breath and drew a halting one. "I'm ready to be a tourist," I told Luca, earning a grin from his sexy lips. "And just be with you."

"Good," he murmured, sealing his lips to mine.

Yes, today...I was Luca's.

Tomorrow? I wasn't going to think about that.

CHAPTER TWENTY-TWO

Luca

NESTLED AGAINST ME, Katherine drowsed in the hotel bed after a long day at the Coppola vineyard. She had been delighted to learn everything about the wine-making process on the private tour, even though the filmmaker hadn't been our tour guide.

Watching her eyes light up had been worth every inconvenience the trip had caused to my work schedule. I hadn't planned to spend so much time wooing Katherine, but I couldn't deny that I'd enjoyed every minute. I should've been doing this months ago.

Maybe I'd been scared to get too close. Maybe I'd been caught up in my own arrogance—the Donato way striking again.

Either way, I was man enough to admit I'd gone about it all wrong and now I was faced with damage control. I wanted to wake up with Katherine by my side every morning. I wanted to taste her kiss and swallow her cries for the rest of our lives. Falling in love with your arranged wife… I guess it wasn't the usual thing, but I didn't care. I loved Katherine and I had to find a way to convince her that I was being genuine.

Today had been a good start.

Katherine sighed in her sleep, her hand curled under her chin.

As if sensing I was having a good moment, my father called.

I hesitated, tempted to send him to voice mail, but I eased myself away from Katherine and out of the bedroom to take the call.

"What's the status?" Giovanni asked gruffly. No hello, no *how are you*, just plain business. I'd long since stopped hoping my father would find his humanity in old age, but I knew Dante still hungered for that fatherly affection and that was a constant irritant between us. I'd settle for respect. I wanted to grab Dante and say, *Open your eyes, you idiot*, but Dante was as stubborn as a Donato could be, so I didn't waste the energy.

"I'm making progress."

"What does that mean?" Giovanni asked, irritated. "Are you bringing her home or not?"

"She's not a piece of luggage," I said, matching my father's clipped tone. "Don't worry about my fiancée. I have everything under control."

"I'm going to call her father, have him bring her to heel. I need you here, not chasing after some silly twit."

"Watch your mouth, old man."

"Have you forgotten who you're speaking to?" Giovanni shot back in warning, but I didn't care. I was tired of my father bullying everyone around him. Times were changing, yet Giovanni was anchoring the family to an antiquated and frowned-upon tradition. I mean, Jesus, we weren't in feudal Italy any longer. "Mind your own business. I have things handled."

"I want details."

"Details? What the hell does that mean?"

"How do you have things *handled*?" Giovanni replied, his disbelief evident.

My father was the last person I would accept relationship advice from. He and my mother were strangers to each other, and it seemed they preferred it that way. My mother was content to doodle around, lunching and gossiping with her matron hens, and my father was off trying to remain in the power seat when he should've retired years ago. I was sick of his bullshit.

"Just back off," I told him, ready to get off the phone.

"You forget your place," Giovanni said, unimpressed with my stance. "I want you on the next flight home."

"I'm not leaving without Katherine. I'll be home when we come together."

"Don't be stupid. I should've found you a different girl, a better one, two years ago. One girl is not worth this much trouble."

This one was. "Don't talk about things you know nothing about. Just keep your nose out of my business and we'll be fine. Cross that line…and you're no longer my father."

The silence on the other line was deafening. Would Giovanni get the message that I wasn't playing around? I wouldn't let anything come between Katherine and me. Never again. "You might have introduced her into my life, but she was meant to be mine, so back off and leave me to my business."

"You love her?" he asked, shocking me with the bald question.

"Isn't it obvious?" I answered.

He exhaled in irritation, but he didn't question me further. I hadn't made a conscious choice to defy my father, but the time had come. My father was the kind of man who would push for as long as someone allowed him. That time was done.

"So when are you coming home?" Giovanni asked by way of concession.

"In a few days. I'll be at the office on Monday."

"I suppose that'll do."

"It's the only offer on the table."

There was a long pause, and then my father said, with uncharacteristic paternal concern, "I just want what's best for the family."

"Then trust that I will do what needs to be done to protect the Donato name, but you have nothing to fear from Katherine. She's going to make a fine Donato."

Giovanni harrumphed as if to say, *That remains to be seen*, and then said, "I'll see you Monday."

The line went dead and I clicked off.

A sound caused me to turn. Katherine leaned against the doorjamb, dressed in a T-shirt and nothing else—just the way I preferred her, actually, but her expression was questioning. It didn't take much brainpower to realize she'd heard at least part of the conversation.

"Who was that?" she asked.

"My father."

"What's going on?"

I could level with her—take the chance that she could handle the ugly truth—or I could lie.

The urge to smooth things over with a lie was strong, but I knew if I was going to make a fresh start with Katherine, I had to start with complete honesty.

"My father wanted me to come home. I told him I wasn't ready."

"Does he need you back at the office?" she asked with a confused frown. "I didn't think Giovanni needed anyone, the way he seems to be in control of everything."

"He likes to think he's in control," I corrected her with a small smile. "But he's not in control of this time between us right now. I'm dying to know what you have in store for us today."

Since I'd taken over half of her day yesterday, it was her turn to plan the activities. Somehow I doubted we were heading to another soup kitchen, but as long as I was with her, I'd board a ship to the moon if that was where she wanted to go.

If she was charmed by my answer, she didn't let on. I knew she wanted more details about my conversation with my father, but I wasn't going to let anything ruin our day.

"So what's it going to be?" I asked.

Realizing the subject was finished on my end, Katherine pursed her lips, disappointed, but took my cue. "Today we are cleaning kennels," she answered, watching for my reaction.

"Kennels...for dogs?"

"Yes. There's a rescue group for sled dogs, and they always need volunteers to help brush the dogs, feed and walk them, as well as just socialize with them."

"So, we're going to play with dogs today?" I clarified, just making sure I had the way of things. At her nod, I said, "All right, then, jeans, tennis shoes and a hoodie."

Maybe she expected pushback, because I'd never been all that into dogs, but it wasn't going to happen. Besides, how hard could it be to play around with a few of them?

"I'm ready when you are," I said, taking the opportunity to steal a quick kiss. She gasped and tried not to smile, but her futile attempt at seeming stern was laughable…and cute. I released her so she could get dressed, and she scuttled back to the bedroom, closing the door behind her.

As if that would stop me from totally undressing her in my mind every second of every day.

For the rest of our lives.

CHAPTER TWENTY-THREE

Katherine

LUCA HAD STOOD up to his father—that much I'd gathered—but there was something else…something that'd caused Luca to growl at his father like a wolf, and that was a side of Luca I'd never seen.

I bit my lip as I leaned against the closed door, processing what I'd heard and what Luca had shared.

Luca had always done his best to be the dutiful son. He bore the weight of his family's expectations without complaint, but something his father had said had made Luca openly bristle.

Had Luca been defending me?

I frowned in thought. What could Giovanni have said to make Luca react like that? I guess it didn't matter, but Luca's reaction created a chain reaction in my thoughts that felt suspiciously like pride.

Luca was more than capable of handling himself in the business world; he didn't need Giovanni shadowing his every move any longer, yet he tolerated his father's influence.

Except today.

Today, he'd stood up to Giovanni and basically told the old curmudgeon to back off.

For me.

A warm, cozy, tingly feeling crept from my belly to my heart.

And now we were going to Nor-Cal Rescue to play with fluffy dogs. I couldn't imagine a better start to the day.

I dressed quickly, and by the time I exited the bedroom, ready, Luca had already ordered an Uber to pick us up. Before we left the room, he teased, "Should I prepare for another hostel experience, or shall we be staying here for the duration of our trip?"

"Kiss my butt, you know the answer to that," I said, shaking my head with a small laugh. "I don't want to stay in another hostel, thank you very much. And screw you for making me realize that I'm not cut out to be a boho hipster. You dashed my dreams, Luca."

His eyes lit up at my teasing. Our playful banter was something I'd sorely missed, even if I was loath to admit it.

When he slipped his hand into mine, I didn't pull away.

We arrived at Nor-Cal Rescue, a small shelter run by volunteers and kept afloat by donations, and were greeted by the coordinator, Emmett George, an affable man with twinkly eyes and a bushy beard.

I shared a look with Luca, knowing we were thinking the same thing—Emmett was the people version of a husky.

I liked him immediately.

"The lady here says you two are from New York…
Business or pleasure?" he asked, looking from me to
Luca with an engaging smile. "Either way, it's right
decent of you to volunteer some of your time with our
pups."

Yips and yelps echoed in the background, and I
smiled, eager to get started. I'd always wanted a husky,
but my father hadn't been interested, so I never got the
chance.

When I discovered there was a rescue group in San
Francisco, I knew there was no way I was leaving without cuddling with some big fluffy dogs.

Luca, far less animal crazy than me, looked just as
excited as I was to help out, and that only intensified
the confusion in my heart.

There were no easy answers between us—I should
probably stop looking—but in the meantime, I was
going to give myself permission to simply enjoy the day.

Emmett brought us into the compound, a clean but
small space where every kennel was occupied by some
type of northern breed, from Siberian husky to malamute.

And they were all freaking gorgeous.

"How could anyone abandon a dog like this?" I asked
as Emmett leashed a beautiful red husky with eyes as
blue as Luca's. "She's amazing."

"She's a runner," Emmett explained with a sigh as he
hooked up a fluffy malamute for Luca. "This purebred
lady is an escape artist. Apparently, her previous owners couldn't keep her occupied and she got bored. And

when huskies get bored, they find mischief. In Cora's case, the owners gave up and surrendered."

I made a sad face. "That's awful."

"Well, some people see a husky or northern-type breed and all they think is 'Wow, pretty dog,' with no thought as to how the breed must be cared for. The overwhelming crime for each of these dogs is that their previous owners simply didn't know what they were getting into when they purchased from the breeder."

Animals were my weakness. I wanted to throw gobs of money at the shelter to ensure that the pups remained safe and cared for. As if keying in on my desperate desire, Luca said, "I'd love to make a donation, if I could."

"We never turn down cash," Emmett said, smiling. "Feeding these hungry beasts doesn't come cheap. We feed the pups a grain-free diet, as most get skin allergies from that crap that most people feed their dogs. Not here, though. Nothing but the best. Hell, sometimes I even go without just so these beautiful rascals get a good meal."

"It's official, I love you," I said to Emmett, casting a glance at Luca, who was chuckling. "You are an incredible human being to give so freely of your time and resources. Yes, please, let us leave you with a donation. It's the least we can do."

"Sounds like a plan to me. Why don't you take Cora and Togo for a walk, and when you come back, I'll have the paperwork drawn up for your donation. It's tax deductible, you know." He fake whispered to me, "I always try to tack that on so that people feel free to be generous."

I laughed, knowing that Luca would probably be ridiculously generous, and I was grateful for his willingness to reach into his pocketbook, even if it was only to score points with me.

We set out with a brisk pace, which helped mitigate the bite in the foggy air. The city was certainly not sunny today, not that the dogs minded one bit. For the pups, this was perfect weather.

Togo, the malamute, was leading pretty hard, but I was impressed with how Luca handled the big dog. My dog, Cora, was more playful than anything else, wanting to sniff and investigate everything, turning to look at me every now and again with a doggie smile.

"They are pretty cute," Luca admitted as our dogs kept pace with each other. "Let me guess, you want one."

"And if I did?"

"Then we'd leave with a dog, I suppose."

Luca made everything sound so simple.

Want a dog? *Get one.*

Don't like your career? *Get a new one.*

Love me? *Get married.*

I withheld my response. I was utterly confused about where to go from here, but if I decided to back out of the contract and stay in California, I had no doubt that my father would cut me off, leaving me penniless.

Knowing that, I really shouldn't bring a dog into my life, but there was something about Cora that I couldn't quite shake.

But there was also something very appealing about how easily Luca took to the pups.

"Did you ever have a dog?" I asked.

He laughed. "No. Mother wouldn't hear of it. The thought of an animal loose in her home? She'd rather die. But I never felt the need to have a dog, either. I guess I'm ambivalent about animals."

"My dad wouldn't let me have a dog, either. But unlike you, I always wanted one. Dogs are amazing. They never judge you, and they're always happy to see you. How can you not love that?"

He shrugged. "Guess I never gave it much thought."

"So, even though you aren't really into dogs, you were willing to do this with me today?"

"Katherine, I would do anything you asked. Spending time with you is all that matters, whether it's in a private sex club or a soup kitchen filled with homeless people. You are the only factor that matters in the scenario."

Tiny flutters tickled my heart. Togo whined and immediately found a spot to poop. I burst out laughing at Luca's chagrined expression. I fished out a plastic poo bag from my pocket and handed it to him.

Togo, finished, glanced up at Luca, very proud of himself.

"I feel ya, buddy. That's how I feel after a good poop, too," he said, causing me to laugh harder. Luca flashed me a quick grin before scooping up the pile and throwing the bag in the nearest trash can. "That might be why I never felt the need to get a dog," he admitted as I wiped my eyes, still giggling.

I looked to Cora, wondering if she was going to

follow suit, but she seemed ready to resume our walk without relieving herself.

We walked a few more blocks, admiring the architecture, sharing likes and dislikes, until we returned to the shelter, where Emmett had a few new jobs for us.

"Oh, goody, more poop," Luca remarked wryly as we started cleaning out kennels while Emmett took the rest of the dogs to the small yard to stretch their legs a bit. Luca paused to rest on his shovel. "If I did have a dog, I would feel zero guilt hiring someone to handle the dirty work."

"I would be okay with that," I admitted, wrinkling my nose at the odors in the room. "This is a little more than I bargained for."

"Big dogs, big poops."

I laughed again. "Yes, that seems to make sense."

We finished up in the kennels, and Emmett funneled the dogs back into their cages. It broke my heart to see such beautiful dogs stuck in cramped little cells. "It's like prison for dogs," I said with a sad face.

"That's exactly how I see it, too," Emmett agreed, but there wasn't much he could do to change the situation. He was doing the best that he could with what he had. "But our goal here is to find forever homes for these pups, so this is a temporary pit stop to wherever they're going to end up. We never put a dog down, but we are limited in our space, so we can only take the dogs that are easy enough to rehome."

"Careful, Emmett, you'll have my softhearted fiancée offering to build you a new structure to house all the poor, abandoned and neglected dogs in San Francisco."

Emmett laughed, seemingly oblivious to the fact that he was standing next to one of the wealthiest men in the world. What good was all that wealth if you couldn't put it to good use? "If you were to build a new compound, where would you build it?" I asked, curious.

Luca just shook his head, knowing the direction my thoughts were traveling.

"Ah, hell, I don't know. Hard to say with real estate prices the way they are here in the city. I haven't even looked. Don't want to put my energy toward something that will never happen. But before I start sounding like a downer, we do all right here. We have some pretty generous donors that keep Nor-Cal Rescue alive, so I'm not complaining."

I seriously loved this man. So kindhearted and humbled by every blessing. I looked to Luca, practically begging him with my eyes to make this man's dream come true.

"Can I get a business card?" Luca asked with a small sigh, and my smile widened.

Emmett fished around in a pocket and found the saddest, most crumpled-up excuse for a card and handed it to Luca with a chagrined expression. "No one ever asks for business cards. I just keep that one in my pocket so I don't forget our 501(c)3 identification. Sometimes our donors want that info right away."

Luca hesitated. "If you need to hold on to it…"

"No, you keep it. I needed to get a fresh one out of my office at some point anyway. Besides, in light of that sweet donation and your time, I think I can let loose of one card."

I shared a secret smile with Luca as he pocketed the card and looked to me. "Are you ready to go, sweetheart?"

I took one last lingering look at Cora and Togo, hoping with all my heart they found loving homes soon, and nodded. I didn't even mind Luca using the endearment; my heart was filled with sap and goo.

We walked to the awaiting Uber and climbed in.

Sweaty, smelly and starving—but I couldn't imagine a better day.

Maybe I'd been wrong to assume things about Luca.

He'd spent this entire time with me, without complaint, just to show me that he was different.

That I was worth the trouble he was willing to face by refusing to leave me behind.

A suspicious tingling tickled my nose. Luca misinterpreted my emotion as sadness for the dogs, pulling me close to say, "Don't worry, those dogs will find excellent homes. I'll see to it, I promise."

I barked a watery chuckle and buried my face against his chest. I wished concern for the dogs was the reason for my sudden urge to bawl. *Stop being so damn amazing*, I wanted to shout, but I didn't. Instead, I just let him believe that was the reason and simply nodded.

"Thanks for being so generous with your donation," I said, finding my voice again.

I heard Luca's smile as he said, "What can I say? I'm a sucker for a pretty redhead with a soft heart."

I laughed and rested my head against his shoulder.

Yeah, and I was a sucker for the sexy Italian who'd stolen my heart when was I just seventeen.

But I wasn't going to admit it...at least not yet.

CHAPTER TWENTY-FOUR

Luca

WE RETURNED TO the hotel, showered and ordered room service.

I was surprised Katherine hadn't dragged us to some farm-to-table restaurant where we had to slaughter our own chicken or something, but she seemed content to ease up on her attempts at pushing me away.

I wasn't going to look a gift horse in the mouth, but I could fairly feel the weight of her thoughts.

I tilted her chin to brush a soft kiss across her lips.

She gazed up at me, a wealth of unsaid words shining in her eyes. How could I get her to see that I wanted nothing more than to make a life with her?

"What did your dad say to upset you?" she asked.

I knew she'd heard more than she let on. I didn't really want to have this conversation, but I supposed there was no point in running from it if I wanted to start fresh with Katherine.

"He was going to call your father to pressure you into marrying me."

"That wouldn't have worked," she said, scooting up to face me, a stormy frown marring her expression. "I'm not afraid of my father. When I left, I'd already factored in the reality that he would cut me off. As long as I was free from living under anyone's thumb, I was willing to take the risk."

"I don't care if it would've worked or not—I don't want you to marry me like that. When you say *I do*, I want you to say it because you want to."

Katherine softened a little, almost against her better judgment. She was fighting a battle within herself, but I had no idea if I would end up on the victor's side.

"I meant what I said," I told her in earnest. "All that matters is you and me. I would do anything to make you happy."

"Even if it meant walking away from your family?" Katherine challenged, watching me closely. "C'mon, Luca, you know that's not even possible. You're the heir to the Donato empire. Your father would never let you walk, not for any reason."

If she were asking for the moon, I'd find a way to give it to her.

"You mean more to me than anything money can buy. If that means I step down as my father's heir and walk away from everything I've ever known to live in squalor, as long as I have you...I'll have everything I'll ever need."

Katherine blinked suddenly as a dam broke. She said with a watery chuckle, "You living in squalor? I can't even picture that. For that matter, how would *I* fare living that way when I could barely stomach the hostel?"

"I have my doubts," I agreed, wiping away her tears gently, "but I'd follow wherever you go."

"I'm so confused," she said, shaking her head. "Everything in me says this will never work, but I have to admit...this week with you has challenged everything I thought I knew about who you are."

"Do you love me?" I asked with blunt seriousness. "Do you? It's very simple."

"It's anything but simple," she disagreed with a scowl. "Nothing about *us* is simple."

"It is to me."

"How is it that you can see so clearly when I feel as if I'm peering through mud?"

"Because I know what matters."

"What about your family?" she asked, unsure, but there was something about her faltering tone that gave me hope.

"Fuck them."

She sucked in a surprised breath. "What about your father?"

"He's an old man. It's time for him to retire and butt the fuck out of my business," I growled.

Stunned, Katherine stared. "Really?" she asked, her voice barely above a whisper. "You would do that?"

"Losing you would be the end of me. What do I need with all that material stuff if I'm broken inside? You are my heart."

Suddenly, the mud Katherine had bemoaned cleared, and I knew something had shifted for her. She could finally hear me. I dared to hope. I grasped her hands and kissed both softly. "Marry me...Katherine."

I held my breath, knowing this was the moment that would make or break everything. I'd never questioned her love for me. Even though she tried, I'd always known her heart was with me. I'd just needed her to realize it, too.

Was it finally happening? Was I stupid to hope?

Just as the moment stretched painfully long and sweat began to dampen my forehead, a tremulous smile formed around the words as she answered with a happy shake of her head. "Y-yes, Luca. Yes, I will marry you."

Thank God. "You've just made me the happiest man on the planet," I said without exaggeration before sealing my mouth to hers. As our tongues twined and danced, I drank in the future with her by my side. I would always support her dreams and goals. If she wanted to go back to school to be a veterinarian, I would be her biggest champion. Whatever she wanted, I would make happen.

A weight of epic proportion fell from my shoulders as she flung her arms around me, hugging me tightly. I could melt into her, losing myself in the sweetness of what I'd cherish for the rest of our lives.

"Luca," she gasped, closing her eyes as I pulled her panties free to sink between her thighs, ready to seal our union with my tongue and breath, but she stopped me, her hand gripping my hair, her expression serious. "Don't ever make me regret this decision," she warned, and I knew exactly what she was saying.

"The next starlet who wants to sit on my lap can sit on the floor," I promised with a crooked grin, and she released my hair.

"Good boy," she said, gesturing with a wide smile. "Continue with what you were about to do."

I laughed and then set about turning her inside out in ways only I could. Until the day I died, the sound of her gasping in pleasure would forever be the greatest gift she could ever give me.

I was the luckiest man alive to have Katherine Oliver by my side.

And I would never forget it.

EPILOGUE

"You sure you're ready to do this?" Nico asked, adjusting my tie, looking to me for confirmation that I wasn't going to ditch my bride and run on cold feet from the Gothic Catholic church. The bells rang out through the city, announcing a Donato was tying the knot.

I smiled at my little brother without a hint of jitters or nerves. For the first time ever, I felt 100 percent sure that what was happening was right.

"Nic, she's everything I ever wanted before I knew what I wanted."

Nico grinned ruefully, saying with a lifted brow, "I have no idea what that means, but if that dopey smile on your face is any indication that you're ready...I guess you are. You look drunk, by the way—and by God, if you say *drunk on love*, I'll fucking vomit."

"I hope you get to experience what I'm feeling right now someday."

"No, thanks," Nico said with good humor. "I'm not the marrying kind. No offense to your girl, but I need more variety than one woman for the rest of my life."

"When you find the right woman, a lifetime spent with her will never be enough."

"I'll take your word for it."

Dante appeared, his hard expression barely softening as he said, "It's time." I'd hoped that Dante would loosen up after our father retired, but if anything he was more wound up than ever, and we'd gone head-to-head more than once at the office.

But today was about my bride, and Dante, at the very least, respected that boundary, even if he looked like he'd sucked a lemon before donning his tuxedo.

I laughed and clapped Nico on the shoulder. "Let's go make an honest man out of me."

"That would take an act of God, and I really don't think anyone checked that off on the gift registry. But, hey, we can at least manage hitching you to one fine woman. How's that?"

"Sounds good to me." I tugged at my jacket sleeves, ensuring everything was perfect, and exhaled slowly. "Let's do this."

I walked with my brothers, ready to marry the woman of my dreams, and I was struck by an incredible sense of gratitude. I could've lost her. Someone must've been on my side, because there was a moment when the scales could've tipped the other way. I shuddered to think of how things could've gone wrong.

Everything had worked out—that was all that mattered.

We took our places at the front of the church, Father Gabriel smiling. Familiar faces stared back at me, some smiling, some not. A Donato wedding was a spectacle for East Coast society. Everyone sitting in a pew was among a select few, and some wore their smug satisfaction as surely as their girdles holding every bit of flesh in their designer clothes.

The popular bridal song "Canon in D" by Pachelbel began and everyone turned as Katherine, my incredible lady, appeared, a vision in cloud white, a gown fit for a queen.

The crowd murmured at her beauty, stunned by the upswept red hair, blazing tendrils caressing her porcelain face, a dainty tiara perched on top.

My heart swelled with so much love, tears sprang to my eyes.

But fuck it, I didn't care who saw me cry.

My eyes were locked on her.

Life was too good to be true.

My father had retired, and with him went his old-school ways. I was in the process of rooting out the lingering aftertaste of his archaic policies, and I'd burned any evidence of my soon-to-be-wife's contract.

Katherine was my equal—my partner—she chose me as much as I chose her.

And she was pregnant.

We weren't telling anyone just yet. The baby was our little secret.

She fucking glowed.

I couldn't wait to carry her over the threshold of our new place—a modest house we'd picked out together—that was a far enough drive from the Donato estate to create a buffer, but not so far that my mother would squawk about not being able to see her new grandchild.

A tiny shiver skipped down my back, and Nico caught the subtle movement. "You okay?" he murmured, shooting me a worried look. "You got this?"

I responded with a slow, sure smile. Oh, yes, I had this—and I was never letting go.

* * * * *

LET'S TALK
Romance

For exclusive extracts, competitions
and special offers, find us online:

f facebook.com/millsandboon

⊙ @millsandboonuk

𝕏 @millsandboon

Or get in touch on 0844 844 1351*

For all the latest titles coming soon, visit
millsandboon.co.uk/nextmonth